WIND CHILL

A StormWatch Novel

RITA HERRON

BEACHSIDE READS

Wind Chill

Beachside Reads READS|

Beachside Reads, Norcross
GA 30092

Print Edition ISBN: 9781706170594
Digital Edition AISN: B07YLY99DP
First Edition 2019, Printed in the USA
10 9 8 7 6 5 4 3 2 1

DEDICATION

To Deb, Peggy, Vicki, Regan and Cindy —I'm honored to be among you amazing authors with this special project!

WIND CHILL

TINLEY 7 NEWS

Bailey Huggins hated the cold, but she had a job to do, and today that meant braving the elements to do it. People had to be informed and warned about the blizzard bearing down on the state and its inherent dangers or else they might get caught out in it.

The cameraman motioned for her to stand in front of the "Welcome to Tinley" sign so he could capture the wind battering it and the power lines as they swayed beneath the force.

She did as he instructed, then yanked her snowcap tighter over her ears, already chilled to the bone. But she was a professional trying to work her way up at the station, so as she waited to begin the segment, she pasted a smile on her face.

Rick gave her the cue, and she raised her voice so it could be heard over the roaring wind, "This is Meteorologist Bailey Huggins, reporting to you via Channel 7 news, Tinley, Nebraska. As of midnight last night, a severe weather advisory has been issued for the entire state. Holly, the worst blizzard to strike in eighty years, has already wreaked havoc on

Montana and Colorado, leaving fatalities and devastation in its wake."

Thick snowflakes pummeled her, but she brushed them from her eyes with a gloved hand. "Temperatures have already dropped into the single digits and are expected to land below zero by morning, with the wind chill reaching thirty below in the next twenty-four hours." She shivered, struggling to keep her teeth from chattering.

"Road advisories have been issued, flights have been cancelled across the Midwest, and power outages are already being reported."

She paused for dramatic effect. "This is no joke or laughing matter. Everyone is urged to stay inside and off the roads for their own safety. Make sure you have emergency supplies available, along with food and water. Once the storm hits, roads may be impassable, businesses closed, and you won't be going anywhere."

She paused again, this time adding a small smile. "Happy Holidays, folks. Unfortunately though, our White Christmas is just about to get nasty."

CHAPTER ONE

SPECIAL AGENT GIA FRANKLIN was on TV again. Talking about *him.*

A smile curved his lips as he studied her smoky amber eyes, now filled with distrust and determination as she addressed the press conference.

The Fed was proving to be a worthy adversary. Strong-willed and smart. Calm, yet menacing in the way she stared down the reporters who tossed questions at her like live grenades.

He felt like he knew her. Like she was becoming a friend. Maybe he'd forget the formalities and just call her Gia.

Just as he'd wanted to do all those years ago when she'd ignored him.

She wasn't ignoring him now.

Gia thumped her fingers on top of the podium. "I'm sorry to report that there are now nine victims of the Christmas

Killer." A photograph of the latest female to die at his hands flashed on the screen.

Only this was a plain picture of her, not the way they'd found her. The beautiful red scarf he'd wrapped around her neck and the ornament he'd lovingly tied to her wrist were missing.

"This is Terry Ann Igley, age twenty-seven. She owned a pet grooming and boarding service that catered to tourists in Gulf Shores, Alabama," Gia continued. "If you have any information regarding her murder, please call your local police or the FBI."

His blood stirred at the memory of Terry Ann's pretty dark eyes pleading with him not to kill her. She had a tender spot for all live creatures, especially dogs and cats, and was organizing a pet parade where owners dressed their furry friends in holiday costumes.

She'd trusted him.

Until she hadn't.

"When are you going to catch this guy?" a blond reporter in the front row asked.

Gia glanced at the male agent next to her, but he simply gestured for her to answer the question. It was obvious she was in charge.

"We are doing everything within our power to identify the perp and stop his killing spree. Since he has struck now in three different states, the FBI has formed a joint task force with law enforcement agencies across the states."

"He started in your home state of Florida, didn't he?" a dark-haired male reporter prodded.

The agent hesitated. Because she wasn't from Florida. Gia Franklin grew up in the small town of Tinley, Nebraska. She'd moved to Florida after she'd joined the Bureau.

She had one sibling, a sister named Carly, who still lived in Tinley, aka Tinsel Town, because each year the town hosted a huge holiday festival with activities and decorations that drew tourists from all over the region.

Carly was blonde and beautiful with the hair and face of an angel. So opposite of her ice-queen sister.

"Florida is my home now," Gia said instead. "And yes, the first three victims were from the south Florida area, then the assailant struck next in Georgia."

The raven-haired reporter waved her hand. "Three murders in Florida, three in Georgia and now three here in Alabama. He's left an ornament from the Twelve Days of Christmas song with each victim. That means he's not finished."

The agent lifted her chin, anger radiating from her cool eyes. "Judging from his MO to date, I'd say that's a fair assessment. All the more reason we need anyone with information regarding the victims to come forward. No matter how small the detail, it might be helpful."

Laughter bubbled in his throat at the double meaning of the name they'd given him. *The Christmas Killer*. Fitting that he was destroying the holiday spirit for these do-gooders with his murders. All methodically planned.

His Christmases had been ruined a long time ago.

He glanced at the box of special ornaments handcrafted after the Twelve Days of Christmas song. He'd left the partridge in a pear tree ornament with his first victim. The second, two turtledoves. The third, three French hens. The fourth, four calling birds...

He still had three more ornaments to dole out.

Another reporter cleared her throat. "Agent Franklin, women need to be warned. Do you have a profile of the killer?"

Gia's chest rose and fell on a deep breath, then she curled her fingers around the edge of the podium with a white-knuckled grip.

3

"We believe he's a white male, mid-thirties. He's methodical, organized and wants attention, as if he's staging a show by posing his victims." She swallowed. "He's charming, average to good looks, blends in with a crowd so he often goes unnoticed. In fact, that may be a sore spot with him. He feels he's invisible."

She hesitated, then cleared her throat. "While he may exhibit outward signs of violence, he possesses a dark sinister side and may be suffering from bipolar disorder coupled with manic depression. Most likely, he experienced a traumatic event around this time of year causing the holidays to trigger his rage."

The reporter's hand shot up. "Do you have any idea where he'll strike again?"

She paused as if searching for answers, then stared directly into the camera. "Not at this time. But I promise you I won't stop until I catch him and put him behind bars."

His blood heated with admiration and...anger. Gia Franklin had just challenged him.

A chuckle rumbled from deep in his gut. She wanted to make this personal.

Hell, he'd considered making it personal before. Now he would. He'd make it *very* personal.

He snagged his phone and accessed the airlines' flight schedules. He'd planned to stay in the sunny South for the last three kills.

Now things would change, and he would up the ante. He'd skip a few states and take Gia back home. Then he'd throw her off her game.

"Nebraska, here I come," he muttered as he booked the next flight out.

Adrenaline surged through him, and he picked up another red scarf and brushed it across his cheek.

By tonight, he'd be in Tinley with Gia's sister.

CHAPTER TWO

9:20 A.M. DECEMBER 18, Gulf Shores, Alabama

SPECIAL AGENT GIA FRANKLIN loved her job. But she hated being massacred by the media.

And with nine young women dead, they were out for blood.

How could she blame them though? The Christmas Killer had struck nine times in three weeks. His MO was unique. He was cunning, fast, and so far, he'd left zero evidence behind.

The fear he'd stirred up was a force in itself. Trouble was, no one understood where he'd attack next. Worse, his victimology was all over the place. He had no type. No specific hair color or profession or body type.

All women in their twenties seemed to be fair game.

All young and vibrant with futures to look forward to.

Until he'd strangled the life out of them.

"Well, that went well," Special Agent Brantley Harmon gritted out as they exited the conference room.

Gia gave him a dry look. "People are scared and angry. Can't fault them for that."

"We'll catch him, Gia," Brantley said.

Her throat thickened with emotions, making it difficult to speak. She had to get out of here before she fell apart. Breaking down on the national news certainly wouldn't instill confidence in the public.

She muttered that they'd talk later, then rushed through the door, well aware reporters would hound her. Another round of the vultures stood out front of the courthouse, hungry for details. She darted to the right to avoid them. Cameras flashed as she jogged down the steps and hurried to her rental car.

Her phone buzzed with a message as she slid into the driver's seat. She checked the number, praying it was a tip about the Christmas Killer.

No, not work. Carly instead. God, she loved her sister, but she knew what this phone call was about. They had a similar conversation every Christmas.

But this year she had a good excuse for not returning to Nowhere, Nebraska.

The buzzing ended, then the phone began ringing again. Carly was nothing but persistent. Gia set her computer bag on the floor then connected the call.

"Hey, sis."

"Gia, I'm so glad you answered. I've been thinking about you so much. I was hoping we could finalize Christmas plans."

A wave of nostalgia washed over Gia. Her sister loved Christmas as much as their mother had. When she died, Carly had assumed ownership of Tinsel Town's infamous holiday shop *Happy Holidays*! which remained opened year-round. Her mother had even chosen the special font for the sign because of its cheery look.

Gia had left town and all the hub of Christmas behind shortly after the funeral. There were too many painful memories tied to both.

"Everyone here is busy gearing up for the annual festival, and I'm hoping you'll be here to celebrate this year. I put Mother's poinsettia quilt on the bed for you, but I wanted to wait till you got here to trim the tree –"

"Hold on, sweetie." Gia struggled to keep her tone even instead of reminding her little sister that she hated Christmas now. It was one reason she'd moved to the Sunshine State.

No more freezing winters, small town antics or cheesy Christmas parades.

"Ahh, sis, you don't really hate it. Remember taking family pictures in that big sleigh at the tree farm," Carly said. "We'd laugh and chase each other through the woods pointing out the best trees."

"Only you chose the saddest ones because you felt sorry for them," Gia murmured with a pang of longing for her sister. She squeezed her eyes shut. "There was also that mean little boy who liked to jump out from behind the trees and scare us with an ax."

Carly laughed. "He was weird, but we still had fun. Please tell me you're coming." Emotions laced her sister's voice. "I understand it's difficult, but it's been three years. And it's even harder for me without you here. I wanted to wait to choose the tree with you at the tree farm like we used to do but figured it might be easier if I already had it. I picked a lovely balsam fir instead of a sad one."

Gia smiled, then hardened her heart. "I can't make it, sis." She could not go back to the place where her mother had been so vibrant and welcomed locals and strangers with her homemade hot chocolate and frosted sugar cookies. "I'm sure you've seen the news about the serial killer we're hunting. He started in Florida, then went to Georgia and just strangled three women in Alabama."

"Oh, right, the one who leaves the Twelve Days ornaments tied to his victim's wrist with red ribbon."

"That's him," Gia said, hating that the media practically glamorized his signature. "I just left a press conference. People are panicked and worried. This maniac isn't finished. He's planning more murders."

A long weary sigh. "Of course, your job is important," Carly replied. "But so is family and being together for the holidays, Gia. Sometimes you need to take a break from work and smell the sugar cookies." She paused again, probably hoping for a laugh, but Gia didn't feel like laughing.

"Besides," her sister said, "you'll get a chance to see Murphy. You know he's the sheriff now."

Murphy, aka Murph, Malone was handsome, sexy and darkly brooding. He'd been voted most athletic in school, and he played guitar like a rock star. Every girl in Tinley lusted after him. They'd dated for a short time and she'd lost her heart to him. But he'd broken it off.

She still didn't understand the reason.

She certainly didn't have time for romance now. Besides, Murph would never leave Tinley, and *she* could never live there again.

One of the reporters from the press conference darted down the courthouse steps after the local police chief, and Gia decided it was time to leave so she started the engine of her rental car.

"Maybe after the holidays we can get together. By then, I'll have caught this guy, and you can fly to West Palm. January is perfect weather in Delray Beach. We can sit on the beach, drink martinis and read magazines."

A tense second passed. "I guess I could come, after the Christmas rush."

"See, that'll work. You can escape the brutal winter and work on a tan." Gia sighed. "I heard the weather forecast. A blizzard is heading your way."

"I know," Carly said. "Everyone here is worried about how it will affect the festival."

Not surprising. There was nothing else there to do. For heaven's sake, the planning committee started working on the next year's schedule and line up of activities in January.

Gia veered onto the main road from town and drove toward the hotel where she'd spent the last four nights. "Just be careful, sis. They're predicting a dangerous wind chill factor. Bundle up and stay in. And for heaven's sake, close the shop if you need to. People will survive with a few less decorations. I certainly have."

"Just because you're surviving doesn't mean you're happy," Carly retorted.

"I'm fine." Gia swallowed hard. "Besides, I'm the big sister. I'm the one who's supposed to look after you."

"You worry too much," Carly murmured.

"I can't afford not to," Gia said. The faces of nine dead women haunted her at night and during every waking hour. Her stomach knotted at the idea of another.

If the Christmas Killer stuck to his schedule, three more women would lose their lives before Christmas.

She had less than a week to find him.

The question was—where would he go next?

CHAPTER THREE

8 p.m., December 18, Tinley, Nebraska

HE SAT outside Tinley's holiday shop, painful memories assaulting him as he watched families browse the aisles for gifts and decoration. White lights twinkled along the exterior of the storefront, which was covered with bows, wreaths and garland.

Through the front picture window, colorful ornaments glittered on the giant tree that occupied the center of the store. A train reminiscent of the Polar Express wound around the base where pretty boxes tied with bright ribbons and bows were stacked, as if symbolizing the joy of Christmas morning.

Collectible Santas, angels and snowmen filled the shelves along with dozens of kinds of ornaments. The back corner housed a toy center with books, puzzles, games and other kid-friendly gift items and was occupied now with squealing children pointing out the presents they wanted.

Once upon a time he'd been just like those innocent little

kids. Happy and delighted by the yuletide season. He'd dreamt of waking up to find toy trucks and a shiny red fire engine when he was five. At seven, he'd lusted after a blue bike he'd seen in a store window.

The song "The Twelve Days of Christmas" chimed in his head, a reminder of the game his mother used to play. Each day for twelve days she wrapped a small surprise for him to open.

But when he was ten, the game suddenly stopped on day twelve. "On the twelfth day of Christmas, my mother abandoned me..."

Then his old man had turned his fists on him.

Anger balled inside him at the memory. After a teacher discovered his bruises, he'd been shipped to foster care.

That had been hell, too.

Later, at the community college, he'd met Mary Jo and thought he'd have a family once again.

Only last year three weeks before Christmas, she'd walked out on him, too.

A blustery wind suddenly picked up outside, battering the garland dangling between the light posts. The traffic light, the only one in the Podunk town, swung back and forth with the force as if it might snap off any second.

A damn storm was brewing, just like the weather forecasters had predicted. He hunched deeper into his coat, hating the cold and snow.

If the blizzard struck as expected, it could complicate things.

No...he'd fulfill his mission. He couldn't let Gia down. She was expecting him to make his next move. She just had no idea where he was, or who he planned to grace with the next three ornaments.

The last of the customers left the store, battling wind as they burrowed into their winter coats and ran to their cars.

Snow had already started to fall, coating the street and rooftop in a thin layer of white.

Although signs advertising Tinsel Town's Christmas Festival adorned every streetlamp, with the storm bearing down, the shops were closing early and the streets emptying.

He opened the door to his rental truck, glanced around the street for any stragglers, then decided the area was clear. He searched for security cameras but didn't find any. Lucky him.

But it also seemed odd. It was as if he'd walked back in time when people trusted each other.

Fools.

No one could be trusted.

A bell tinkled above the door as he entered the store. The scent of holiday candles and potpourri wafted toward him. Nauseating.

Gia's sister, Carly, stood behind the counter wearing a bright red Christmas sweater emblazoned with a glittery white snowman. She was bent over, locking the glass cabinet below the counter which held what appeared to be expensive jewelry. Gifts the husbands would rush in to purchase at the last minute when they did their holiday shopping.

Just like he'd done for Mary Jo.

Carly's pale blonde hair was swept up in a ponytail with a bright green ribbon tied around the silky looking strands. They reminded him of corn silk and made his fingers itch to dig into the thick waves.

"Hi, Sir. Welcome to *Happy Holidays!*" Carly walked toward him with a friendly smile. "I'm afraid I'm closing in five minutes. Are you looking for something specific? A gift for a lady friend?"

Not exactly. He'd already purchased his gifts. He was just here to choose the recipients.

His lips curled into what he hoped was a charming smile.

"Or if you need more time, you can come back tomorrow and browse," Carly chirped. "I'll be open at ten."

He stepped closer to her and inhaled the scent of lavender. "I know exactly what I want. It won't take a minute to get it." A second later, he wrapped his arm around her neck and dragged her kicking and screaming toward the rear exit of the store.

CHAPTER FOUR

10:00 P.M., December 18, Gulf Shores Alabama

GIA POUNDED her pillow in frustration. She hadn't slept in two days. But even exhausted, sleep eluded her.

The screams of the dead girls echoed in her ears.

When she closed her eyes, their beautiful gazes, frozen in the shock of death, stared back at her.

She had to stop this madness before he reached a dozen. He could disappear. Or start over again next year.

Her phone buzzed on the nightstand and she snatched it, hoping again for a tip. Carly again.

The last thing she felt like doing was arguing with her sister tonight. She'd thought they had the holiday visit settled. It was just too hard for her to go back to that house. To the bedroom where she'd grown up. To the pictures on the mantle when they were together.

She rolled over and punched the pillow again. But the phone continued to ring. Battling anger and fatigue, she snatched it and connected the call. Before she could speak, a low wail echoed over the line.

"Help me, Gia...please help me!"

"Carly —"

Cold terror swept over Gia as the phone line died in her hand.

10:10 P.M., DECEMBER 18, TINLEY, NEBRASKA

Sheriff Murphy Malone watched the weather report with a growing pit of anxiety in his stomach. With several people already dead in two states from this damn freak blizzard barreling through the Midwest, his town had to be ready.

The media had already warned everyone to stay inside, to stock up, to be prepared to be holed up for days in their houses. Being outside in sub-zero temperatures was not only dangerous.

But also deadly.

He didn't want any casualties in Tinley.

Of course, residents were up in arms over having to cancel the holiday festival plans that generated much needed revenue for the fledgling farm community, but it couldn't be helped. Still, dozens of tourists had arrived early and had filled the local inn and cottages on the creek.

The grocery store aisles were practically empty, the hardware store packed with folks buying batteries, searching for space heaters and back-up generators, and other emergency supplies. Larry's Liquor Store had lines out the door.

The weather forecast ended, and a recap of a morning news clip from Gulf Shores, Alabama came on air. He'd already seen it, but he watched it once more just because

Tinley's own Gia Franklin was the one talking, and he'd always had a thing for her.

They'd even dated a few times in high school, but Gia had made it clear she wanted more than what small-town life had to offer. He'd been tempted to ask her to stay.

But that wouldn't have been fair. Hell, he'd cared too much to expect her to stifle her dreams and live in Tinley.

And he could never leave.

She'd probably found the excitement she craved with the FBI. Although at the moment, despite her striking beauty, she looked more distressed than anything else.

With nine women dead at the hands of one madman, he could understand why. God help them all.

He flipped off the TV, his body tense. Stories like that got to him.

Murder was not the kind of news people should be hearing at Christmas. Good will and cheer and lending a helping hand to your neighbor—that's what the holidays were about.

And the reason he hadn't left the town for the big city and a better paying job.

That and his mother.

God help her, too.

Once upon a time she'd loved the season and had visited the nursing homes to sing carols and pass out warm socks and handmade blankets so those without families wouldn't feel forgotten.

Now she was sitting in an assisted living facility, hardly able to get around, and her memory was slipping.

Pain squeezed his heart, but he inhaled a deep breath.

As much as it hurt to see her health failing, abandoning her would be worse.

He snapped on his holster and gun, then grabbed his coat

and gloves. He'd drive by town and conduct rounds, make sure everyone was tucked in safe for the night.

Tomorrow he'd stop by and take his mother her favorite cookies. He just hoped she hadn't forgotten that she liked chocolate chip.

10:08 P.M., DECEMBER 18, GULF SHORES, ALABAMA

Carly's cry taunted Gia as she jumped from bed and stabbed her sister's number. The phone rang once, then twice.

Then a voice answered. "You want me, Gia. Come and find me."

Sheer terror knifed through her as the phone went dead again. Dear God...was it him? The Christmas Killer?

Did he have her sister?

No, he'd just killed here in Gulf Shores the night before. He couldn't be in Nebraska...

Unless he'd left town right after he'd posed the last body.

Tears blinded her, and she paced the bedroom and punched the number again. This time it rolled to voice mail. "Listen to me, you creep, you touch one hair on my sister's head, and you are dead. Do you hear me? No jail. I will make you suffer then I'll put a bullet in your brain."

She hit disconnect, her mind racing. Denial seized her. He couldn't have her sweet sister. Carly had never done anything to hurt anybody. She loved Christmas and puppies and babies. She wanted to get married and have a family.

She asked you to come home for the holidays and you told her no.

Gia clutched the wall as her legs buckled. The room blurred.

You can't pass out. You have to get to Carly. She needs you.

He said for you to come and get him. He'd taunted her. Maybe he hadn't hurt her sister yet. Maybe there was time...

She latched onto that sliver of hope and raced to her computer. She accessed flight information, searching for the first available flight to Nebraska.

While she waited on the information, she found the phone number for the sheriff's department in Tinley. Her hand trembled as she called the number.

A man's deep gruff voice answered. "Sheriff Murphy Malone."

"Murphy this is Gia Franklin, I'm working a serial killer case."

"I know. I saw the earlier press conference."

She was surprised he'd seen it in the small town. But it was national news. Less explaining to do. "Listen to me. It's about the case. And Carly."

His breath rattled out. "Carly? What's going on?"

A sob caught in her throat, but she swallowed it back. She'd have time to fall apart later. "I just got a call from her begging for help. Then the phone died. When I called back, a man answered." Her voice cracked. "You have to help me, Murph. He—I think the Christmas Killer has Carly."

10:15 P.M., DECEMBER 18, TINLEY

Murphy's heart hammered. "I thought he was in Alabama, that he just struck in the South."

"Time of death for the woman was last night," Gia said. "He could have flown out after he murdered his last victim."

Number nine. Judging from this sicko's MO, there would be three more.

In his city?

No. Hell, no. Tinley was all neighbors and Midwestern hospitality.

Gia had to be mistaken. "Did he identify himself as the Christmas Killer?"

"Not exactly, but he said, 'You want me. Come and get me.'" She hissed. "He was watching the press conference."

"It could be a prank. You know tip lines bring out crazies and false leads and—"

"The call came to my personal cell number directly from Carly's phone. I heard her voice." Gia's tone sharpened. "She's in trouble."

Murphy raked a hand through his hair, then snagged his keys and headed to the door. "All right. Tell me what you need me to do."

"I'm on the first flight I can get," she said. "But it will take me hours to reach Tinley. I need you to go to Carly's house and see if she's there. And the shop...Check both of them."

"I'm on the way out the door now," Murphy said. "I'll canvas both places and look around town then call you back."

A flurry of commotion sounded in the background, and he assumed she was packing and getting dressed. Gia was right. It would take hours for her to get here.

If she made it. With the weather turning ugly, the airport might even shut down. Flights across the country had already been canceled in staggering numbers. People were stranded in Montana and Colorado with no quick end in sight, causing a domino effect across the states.

"A blizzard is expected to strike Nebraska, with heavy snowfall starting in the morning. If you don't make it—"

"Don't worry. I'll make it," she snapped. "Now get over to my sister's house. I'm headed to the airport."

She sounded panicked. Desperate. Not at all the calm agent she presented in front of the camera. This case had to be wearing her down. The whole country had been following this madman's rampage. "I can call ahead and book you a rental car at the airport," he offered as he slid into his squad car and started the engine.

"No, I'll do it," she said, her tone even sharper this time. "Just find Carly."

Murphy flipped on the siren as she ended the call, his pulse jumping. What if she was right and the Christmas Killer had come to Tinley?

He veered down the side street leading out to the Franklin house. Carly had not only taken over running Beverly Franklin's store, but she'd moved into the family homestead, a rambling old white farmhouse that sat on the edge of the town.

Mrs. Franklin had been vibrant and friendly and volunteered for every festival and event that Tinley boasted. At the first town meeting he'd attended after he had to put his mother into a memory care home, he'd admitted he didn't plan on decorating for the holiday, so she'd brought over Christmas decorations and a tree from the Boy Scout lot and personally trimmed it herself. Her holiday cheer and enthusiasm for the parade and festivities had hacked away at his bah humbug attitude.

Carly reminded him of her mother. Gia...Special Agent Franklin...was a different story though. She had been away at the academy when he'd been elected sheriff. When Beverly had suddenly died of a heart attack, she'd rushed home for the funeral.

The moment he'd seen her, he'd been drawn to her again. Had wondered things had been different, if she might stay. Want him.

He'd itched to console her, but she'd been in shock and grief stricken. And for all he'd known, she had a boyfriend or lover waiting on her where she lived.

Shortly after the funeral, she'd hopped a plane out of town

and had never been back. He'd heard Carly talk about missing Gia at the holidays and wondered how Gia could just abandon her sister.

Although judging from the fear in Gia's voice, it wasn't because she didn't love Carly.

Siren wailing, he sped as fast as the already icy roads allowed, hoping the meteorologists had it wrong this time. The snowfall was light now, only a couple of inches of accumulation, although the wind was roaring like a lion, and the temperature had already dropped to the teens.

A blizzard would cause all kind of mayhem for tourists traveling to Tinley. Some of the small businesses depended on the revenue from the festival to make it through the year financially.

At least most everyone had chosen to stay in tonight and traffic was minimal. Seconds later, he veered into the drive for the Franklin house, his brakes screeching.

He cut the engine and scanned the property. Except for a lone light burning in a back room, the house was pitched in darkness.

Keeping in mind that a serial killer might be in there holding Carly hostage, he removed his weapon from his holster and checked it before he inched up to the house. A wrap-around porch boasted a swing and porch rockers, making the house look inviting, like a post card.

But a killer might be lying in wait.

He considered calling for back-up, but there wasn't time. Carly might be in danger.

Slowly he eased up the steps, then peered through the front windows. The curtains were slightly ajar, offering him a view of a living room and kitchen. Both appeared empty.

No movement that he detected.

The wind rattled a loose shutter, and he jerked his head to the side to check the noise. But he didn't see anyone.

Murphy prowled slowly toward the window to the right and looked inside. Again, no movement or sign anyone was inside.

Praying Gia was wrong, and they were dealing with a prank caller, he knocked on the door. "Carly? Are you home?" He held his breath as he waited.

No answer.

A tree limb cracked and banged the side of the house. He scanned the property. Again nothing.

Senses honed, he opened the screened door then turned the doorknob. Locked.

Hopefully that was a good sign.

On the off chance that she was home in bed and the caller had simply stolen her phone and used it to frighten her sister, he knocked again. "Carly, it's Sheriff Malone. If you're here, please let me in."

He tapped his boot as he waited. Seconds ticked by. No answer.

Dammit.

Deciding to check around back, he slogged through the brush and snow to the rear porch, then climbed the steps. He peered inside the window. Everything appeared normal.

No sign of a break-in or struggle.

The house was big. Carly could be upstairs. In trouble.

He picked the lock, then eased the door open. An eerie quiet filled the house, the old wood floors squeaking as he passed through the mudroom to the kitchen. The counters were neat and clean. No food sitting out, as if Carly had made dinner. Nothing disturbed.

Gun braced, he inched through the downstairs, and searched the bathroom and closets, then climbed the steps to the second floor. The first bedroom to the right held a four-poster bed covered in a quilt made of squares of red poinsettias. Christmas towels hung in the bathroom, but the room was empty.

He moved to the next bedroom, the master. An antique iron bed was covered in another quilt, this one in a snowflake pattern. The master bath was empty as well.

At this hour, with bad weather approaching and her store closed, Carly would probably be home.

Yet there were no signs she'd been here tonight.

Maybe she'd gone to a friend's house?

He'd ask Gia if she had any ideas when he talked to her. But first, he'd search the store.

An image of those damn ornaments the killer left with his victim taunted him. Then the faces of the dead girls.

He just hoped to hell he didn't find Carly's body at *Happy Holidays!*

CHAPTER FIVE

11:00 P.M., December 18, Mobile, Alabama

GIA TRIED Carly's phone again before she boarded the plane, but no answer.

Frantic, she called her partner Brantley. His voice sounded thick with sleep as if she'd woken him.

She quickly explained about the phone call. "I'm praying this is just some twisted prank, but I have to fly to Nebraska."

"I'll meet you at the airport." Noises sounded and she realized he was getting out of bed, probably heading to the shower.

"No, I'm already here. They're cancelling flights left and right. With the backlog across the states, the trickledown effect is enormous. Stay there and answer the tip line in case we get a lead." She inhaled. "I phoned the sheriff in Tinley. He's going to Carly's house and her store to look for her. I'll call you after I land."

Without waiting for a reply, she ended the call and

pressed the sheriff's number. Hopefully Murphy would find Carly alive and safe.

The phone rang twice, then he answered. "It's Gia. Did you find my sister?"

"She wasn't at the house, and no signs of a struggle there. I'm on my way to *Happy Holidays!* now."

Panic knotted Gia's insides. Noise from other passengers buzzed around her as the flight attendant announced her flight was boarding. She snatched her computer case and overnight bag and fell into line.

"I'm about to get on a plane. Let me know if you find her." *Please dear God, let him find her.*

"I will," he said gruffly. "Try not to worry."

"This is my baby sister." Gia's voice was a shaky whisper. "I'm supposed to take care of her, and I may have just led a serial killer to her door."

"We'll find her," Murphy assured her. "Call me when you land."

Gia agreed, then handed her ticket to the attendant and followed the trail of passengers onto the plane.

The flight attendant at the door greeted her with, "Happy Holidays!"

She choked back a cry of despair. Holidays had not been a happy occasion since her mother's heart attack.

She couldn't lose her sister, too.

11:15 P.M., DECEMBER 18, TINLEY, NEBRASKA

Murphy sped toward *Happy Holidays!* hoping like hell he could give Gia Franklin good news soon.

But the knot in his gut warned him that she was right. That the CK had come to his town.

26

The snow was starting to thicken, creating a fog across the landscape and forcing him to slow as he approached a turn. Trees swayed and bent as the wind gusts intensified.

Thankfully the streets were practically deserted of cars though.

Remembering that he'd seen Carly with the veterinarian moving to town, he retrieved the vet's number and asked his voice activation system to dial him. Three rings later and a man answered.

"Dr. Whitman speaking."

"It's Sheriff Malone. Have you talked to or seen Carly Franklin today?"

A hesitant pause. "No, I'm on my way out of town to visit family in Arkansas. Is something wrong? Why are you asking about Carly?"

Murphy sucked in a breath. "Her sister phoned me from out of state. She thinks Carly might be in trouble."

"What?" Whitman muttered. "What kind of trouble?"

"I don't know yet, but I went to her house and she's not there. I'm on my way to her shop to see if there are signs of foul play."

The vet's erratic breathing echoed over the line. "Why would someone hurt Carly?"

Murphy didn't want to alarm him with Gia's theory. "I don't know. Just call me ASAP if you hear from her."

"I will, and Sheriff." Static crackled over the line. "I hope you find her."

Murphy hung up, swung his car into an empty spot in front of *Happy Holidays!* and threw the gearshift into park. He pulled his gun as he jumped out and scanned the street.

The interior was dark, the Christmas lights from the street reflected in the front picture window. He paused at the door and peered inside, scanning what he could see of the interior for movement.

Nothing. Everything appeared to be quiet.

Still, Gia's frantic call echoed in his head as he checked the front door. Locked. He strode down the walkway, then through the alley to the back door. No windows back here. The door was locked as well. An old-fashioned crystal door-knob with an outdated key lock. Carly didn't have an alarm system. No one in Tinley did.

They hadn't needed one before.

Heart hammering, he removed his lock picking tool, stooped down, and shined his pen light on the door. As he picked the lock and eased the door open, he scanned the back entrance, then aimed the light into the storage room to the right. Bags of ribbons, bows and colorful gift boxes filled shelves on one wall while boxes of ornaments, decorations and miscellaneous gift items overflowed three others.

He paused to listen for sounds as he moved past Carly's office and into the main part of the building. "Carly? Are you here?"

Silence met his question, the eerie silence at odds with the cheerful holiday decorations occupying every conceivable area. "Carly, if you're here talk to me."

Again, no response.

His boots pounded the rustic wooden floor as he passed the children's section. No one there.

But as he approached the ten-foot artificial fir tree, his boots made a crunching sound. He looked down and spotted what had made the noise. Broken ornaments.

The crystal snowflakes, angels and glass balls lay scattered across the floor, shattered to pieces. Two of the artificial limbs were bent, and the tree tilted precariously to one side as if it had been knocked over.

Or ...as if someone had grabbed at it for control. As if there had been a struggle.

Pulse pounding, he stooped down to examine the area.

Scuffmarks streaked the floor and drops of blood mingled with the broken glass.

He shined his light along the floor to the right and spotted more blood. A thin trail of it leading toward the back exit.

If Gia was right and the Christmas Killer had Carly, she was in grave peril.

This monster hadn't held his victims hostage. He'd killed them quickly and almost immediately.

It might already be too late for Carly.

CHAPTER SIX

11:45 P.M., December 18, Tinley, Nebraska

MURPHY CALLED a crime team to process the store as soon as he found the blood. Then he called his deputy Cody Freedman and asked him to organize a search party.

Alleyways, abandoned houses, barns, the woods, corn-fields—anyplace they could think of where a killer might leave Carly or be keeping her hostage.

His stomach clenched at the thought of that sweet young girl being out there somewhere in the elements with a madman. Or left dead.

But he had a job to do and that meant putting his emotions on hold. The town needed him. Carly needed him.

But most of all, if Gia was right about the CK being here in Tinley, he had to stop him before he took any more lives.

The glass window on the door rattled as a knock sounded. Snow and a freezing wind swirled through the front door as he let the Evidence Response Team inside. "We got here as soon as we could," Rick Mason, the leader of the team said.

"The weather's already turning nasty." He twisted at his mustache. "Stache is freezing and breaking off out there."

The storm blowing in complicated everything, including the search party's efforts. "I know, but thanks for coming. If Carly Franklin has been abducted, every second counts."

While Rick and Sue Lin, the second ERT agent, left their coats and outer gear on the front bench by the door, Murphy described his vision of what he thought had happened inside the store. "The perp probably hovered outside, watching the store. He waited until all the customers left before he made his move. Knowing Carly, she was friendly to the man, then he accosted her." Murphy gestured toward the shattered ornaments on the floor and the crushed packages. "She grabbed at the tree as she struggled, and the ornaments snapped off and broke, and either Carly or both of them stepped on the packages beneath the tree as they fought. Then he knocked her unconscious and dragged her out the back door. Before he left, he turned off all the lights and locked up so as not to draw suspicion."

"Makes sense," Sue Lin agreed.

Rick angled his camera and began photographing the scene. "There's blood, but not a significant amount."

"The Christmas Killer strangled his victims, didn't he?" Sue Lin asked. "So, there wouldn't have been much blood."

"That fits." Rick took picture after picture while Sue Lin began dusting the doorknob for prints.

Careful not to touch anything or step in the blood, Murphy walked around the room searching for forensics the killer might have left behind. If they were dealing with the CK, he probably wouldn't find any. Nine kills. This psycho hadn't escaped detection by being sloppy.

But those scuffmarks looked like a man's shoes. Hell, maybe he'd taken Gia's sister on a whim to torment Gia and he'd made a mistake. "Be sure to print the shoe scuffmarks," he told Rick. "It's a long shot, but at this point, any detail might help us figure out who this guy is."

"Don't worry, we'll be thorough," Sue Lin promised.

Murphy checked his watch, hoping his deputy might have found something.

But he hadn't received any messages.

Something shiny caught his eye from the counter by the cash register. He walked over to examine it, and his breath quickened.

It was a box of ornaments. The Twelve Days of Christmas ornaments.

The first nine were missing from the box. The tenth one was tied to the tiny spruce tree on top of the counter.

Dammit to hell. The Christmas Killer had left them a message. He was here in Tinley.

1:00 A.M., DECEMBER 19, ATLANTA, GEORGIA

With no direct flights to Omaha, Gia found herself on a layover at Hartsfield International Airport. The few passengers waiting with her for the next flight were stretched out in chairs and on the floor in an attempt to sleep.

Her nerves were too frayed to rest. She paced the wall of windows overlooking the tarmac and phoned the sheriff.

"Did you find her?"

"I'm sorry, but not yet." Worry darkened his tone.

"What *did* you find?" she asked, sensing he was holding something back.

"As I said before, she wasn't home and there was no indication of trouble there." He paused, tension rattling between them. "The shop was a different story."

Oh, God, please don't let Carly be dead.

"She wasn't inside, but there were signs of a struggle. Ornaments from the Christmas tree had fallen and were shattered on the floor and the gift boxes beneath were crushed."

Gia leaned against the wall, her lungs straining for air as she remembered another time when she'd found broken ornaments on the floor. The day her mother had her heart attack.

"Gia?"

"I'm here," she said, her breathing choppy. "Go on."

"There was some blood on the floor, but not much. My guess is that Carly cut her hand on the ornaments when she wrestled with her attacker."

A strained second passed. "So, you believe she was abducted?"

"I'm sorry, but it appears that way. There were scuffmarks on the floor indicating a struggle, then more toward the back exit. Door was locked and the lights turned off to make it appear as if the store was simply closed for the evening."

Tears filled Gia's eyes, panic battling with the need to do something -- *anything* to find her baby sister.

"We can discuss the rest when you get here," Murphy said. "My deputy organized a search party and a crew is already hunting for her. The weather may complicate the search, but we're on top of it."

The world blurred around Gia. His words sounded as if they were coming from far away, as if she was spiraling downward into a dark wind tunnel. Outside, a thunderstorm broke loose and a blustery wind rattled the glass. Although it wasn't snowing in Atlanta, thunder and lightning and heavy rain was complicating travel.

Slowly the sheriff's first sentence registered.

She clenched her phone in a white-knuckled grip. "What do you mean, we can talk about the rest when I get there?"

Another hesitation, stirring her anger.

"Listen to me, Murphy Malone, don't you dare hold

back on me! This is my sister, and I want to know everything you know when you know it. Do you understand
me?"

"I got it," he said in a low voice.

"Then tell me the *rest*."

He cleared his throat. "I found a box of ornaments on the
counter by the cash register. An opened box."

Gia shook her head in denial as the truth dawned on her.
"The Twelve Days?"

"Yes," he confirmed gruffly.

"How many were there?"

A heartbeat of silence passed. "Nine were missing.
Whoever took Carly tied the tenth one to the miniature tree
by the register."

"He left me a message." Gia trembled violently as she
sank down onto the floor. She leaned against the wall and
buried her head into her hands.

Outside, the storm raged on. The intercom announced
delayed and cancelled flights every minute. The airline was
working to set up passengers in hotels and rearrange
connecting flights from folks trying to get home to the
Midwest.

She choked back a cry. She might not make it out of
Atlanta tonight. Worse, even if she did get to Tinley, what if
she was too late to save her sister?

2:45 A.M., DECEMBER 19, TINLEY

Murphy hated to be the bearer of bad news, but Gia was
right. She deserved to be informed. She was not only the
victim's sister, but the agent who'd been tracking this serial
killer for weeks now.

If anyone had an inkling about his next move, where he might hold a victim or leave her body, Gia might.

"Keep me posted on any forensics you find, or results in the lab," he told the ERT. "I'm going to check out a few places where the killer might take her."

"Will do," Sue Lin told him. "We'll lock up when we're finished."

They'd already cordoned off the store with crime scene tape, a macabre sight against the twinkling Christmas lights and glittery sign boasting the store's name.

When the town woke up to see *Happy Holidays!* was a crime scene, people would be upset. Already they weren't thrilled about the possibility of canceling the festival, but to think one of their own was in danger and that a serial killer was stalking the women would cause pandemonium.

His mind raced as he returned to his car, phoned his deputy and filled him in. "Have you found anything yet?"

"Afraid not," Cody said. "We checked a couple of abandoned barns on Route 9, but they were empty. Three volunteers are combing the cornfields off Pine Kettle Road, and we've searched the park. But the wind is starting to bear down, and the thick snowfall is making it difficult to see. We can't leave our men out too long in this mess or we'll be dealing with hypothermia."

Dammit, Cody was right. The wind chill was predicted to plunge below zero overnight and continue declining over the next twenty-four hours. So far, Holly was rolling in fast and furious.

"Understood. Let's set up teams and rotate the volunteers to give everyone a rest and a break from the elements. I'll drive out to the old motel on Pitchfork Street and check it out."

This maniac had to seek shelter from the storm himself to

survive. If he hadn't killed Carly yet, he might be holding her until Gia arrived.

His stomach growled, reminding him he'd had an early dinner last night, so he snatched a protein bar from his console and wolfed it down as he started the engine. Thankful the sheriff's department had switched over to SUV's with four-wheel drive, he pulled away from the town square.

Blinding snow forced him to drive slowly as he maneuvered the alleys and side streets, scanning for signs of trouble. Although it was the middle of the night, he phoned Mistletoe Manor, the local B & B.

A groggy-sounding Inez answered. The innkeeper was in her late sixties with a tender soul and friendly demeanor. She loved running the inn and catering to her guests. Word was she was an incredible cook, and she planned special activities for the families at the inn. She was also his mother's friend and visited her regularly.

"I'm sorry to disturb you at this hour, Inez, but it's important."

"What's wrong, Sheriff?"

"Carly Franklin has gone missing."

"Oh, dear, and in this terrible storm. What in the world happened?"

He didn't want to alarm her, but residents would soon learn about Carly's disappearance anyway. Still, he withheld details. "We have teams searching for her, but it's possible there was foul play."

"How can I help, Sheriff?"

"I know there are a lot of tourists already in town. Did any of the guests at the inn strike you as suspicious? Maybe a single man traveling alone who came in last night?"

He heard a rattling sound and realized she was probably

looking for her glasses. She had a habit of losing them wherever she was. "Let me look at the guest registry."

"Thanks, Inez."

Footsteps sounded, and Murphy maneuvered his SUV past the library and town hall. Holiday decorations adorned the streetlights, twinkling lights everywhere. A giant sleigh sat in the front of the park beside the gazebo where Santa visits occurred daily. The horse and buggy carriage that offered carriage rides through town was parked by the pond. Thankfully the animals had already been moved to a barn to wait out the blizzard.

"No single male guests at all. Mostly there are families, and only one checked in yesterday. The Robinsons from Cleveland. They have four children and come every year for the festival. Said it's part of their family tradition."

They might be disappointed this year.

But the town's festival was the least of his worries at the moment. "Alright, thanks for checking. If any of your male guests act strangely, call me."

"Oh, heavens, now you've got me worried."

"Nothing for you to fret about tonight." Inez was too old to fit the victim's profile. All of his victims had been in their twenties. "Get some rest."

He ended the call and drove past Sari's Sweets which boasted peppermint milkshakes and a dozen different kinds of Christmas cookies and pastries, then turned onto Pitchfork Street, named because it led out to acres and acres of cornfields.

The old motel was four miles from town and had fallen into disrepair three years ago when the owner Willie Pickens died in a tractor accident on his brother's farm. Murphy had expected someone else to snap up the property, but it would take a mountain of work to restore it to its potential. And no one wanted the old building, not with the new cabins built on the east side and the cottages by the creek.

The place slipped into view, and he scanned the area. The structure was crumbling, paint peeling, and the roof needed replacing. Unlike the rest of the town, there were no holiday decorations or sparkling lights. The building appeared dark, except...he spotted a dim light in the room on the end.

His pulse jumped, and he cut his lights on his SUV and veered off the side of the road before he reached the parking lot.

After climbing from the vehicle and gently closing the door, Murphy pulled his gun and crept toward the building on foot. He didn't want to alert whoever was in that room that he was coming.

3:00 A.M., DECEMBER 19, TINLEY

Gia was shocked her plane had taken off and landed. According to the flight attendant though, the airlines were trying to accommodate as many as possible before the worst of the blizzard struck full force which was supposed to be within the next twenty-four hours.

Thankfully, she'd managed to secure a rental car before she'd left Gulf Shores, or she would have been out of luck. The airport floor was carpeted with stranded passengers trying to sleep. Others were accepting housing from virtual strangers and others were sharing vehicles. Although some people were frantic to get home and tempers were stretched thin, she'd seen small acts of kindness as well.

Considering she saw the worst of society on the job, the good will was refreshing and reminded her that not everyone was evil.

Wind rattled the windowpanes of the small SUV and battered the sides, forcing her to grip the steering wheel with an iron fist to keep the car on the road. Snowflakes fell in thick white sheets, black ice already creating hazardous conditions on the highway.

She cranked up the defroster and heater, the bitter cold permeating her all the way to her bones.

Carly's plea for help repeatedly echoed in her head as she braved the roads. Every minute seemed like hours. Finally, a sign for Tinley—Tinsel Town—waved back and forth in the wind. Five more miles.

The car hit an icy patch and skidded, and she fought not to run into the ditch. She had to make it to town. Had to find Carly before it was too late.

An ancient pick-up truck barreled around the corner, going way too fast. She yelled at him to slow down. A second later, the driver hit a patch of ice, swerved, then skidded and careened straight toward her.

Gia bit back a scream as she swerved to avoid crashing into him head on. Unable to avoid the black ice, she lost control and the rental vehicle skidded off the road. She braced herself for the impact, but her head snapped forward as the SUV slammed into a giant oak, and the car nosedived into the embankment.

The window shattered on impact. Glass sprayed her face, and the air bag exploded, slamming into her chest. Her head snapped forward, then she saw stars.

She tasted blood just before the darkness claimed her.

CHAPTER SEVEN

3:10 A.M., December 19, Tinley

HE LISTENED to her shallow breathing as she slept.

He itched to turn on a light and watch her more closely, but it was too dangerous. Someone driving by might see the light and find them.

Right now, they were all alone, cocooned in the midst of the biggest snowstorm in Nebraska's history. The soft white snow falling outside painted the earth in a postcard white like a Norman Rockwell painting.

Yet dark thoughts invaded his head. This was a new feeling. To keep his victim alive instead of snuffing out her life immediately.

Adrenaline had surged through him as he'd watched the horror on her face when she'd opened her eyes and realized she had been taken.

Tears had rained down her pretty ivory cheeks, and she'd pleaded with him not to kill her. She'd rattled on and on about the holidays and good will toward others.

He'd smiled and told her she had a little time, but she wouldn't make it to Christmas. That he was waiting on her sister.

That had shut her up. Had made her eyes widen in terror.

Then he'd given her the drugs to make her sleep.

After all, he was bone tired. Last night he'd been up late posing Terry Ann for the police to find. Then traveling was a pain in the neck. He hated being crammed into those tiny airplanes, arms brushing against sweaty bodies that barely fit into the narrow seats. The damn turbulence from the wind had people puking in the aisles, too. A shudder ripped through him. Disgusting.

People had no manners either. Their bodies pressed together like sardines gave off such bad odors that his stomach roiled.

The woman seated next to him on the last leg of the journey had been so paranoid she'd yelped and clutched his arm every time the plane dipped and jolted.

He'd been tempted to put her out of her misery and make her number ten.

But...he couldn't strangle her in public and raise suspicion. Besides, she'd babbled on and on about how her family was waiting. If she didn't make it off the plane alive, all the passengers would be detained and questioned.

He didn't have time for that.

So, he'd tried to calm her, then when she'd raised the shade on the window to look outside at the storm, he'd slipped a pill in her drink and she'd drifted off to la la land for the remainder of the flight.

Finally blessed quiet.

Now Carly...she was a different story. Even frightened, her voice sounded like honey. Her long blonde hair looked like corn silk from the Nebraska fields and her skin was the purest ivory he'd ever seen. A man could lose himself in her sea-blue eyes and the scent of jasmine wafting from her skin.

It was a shame he had to kill her.

But...Gia Franklin had challenged him. And he did not back down from a fight.

Not even for a sweet innocent thing like Blondie.

His heart hammered in his chest. His game had to end soon, but what a way to end it.

The grand finale, two women in one night, sisters no less, and one the very agent chasing him, would make him a legend!

But first...first he had to take one more woman. He'd already chosen her.

For now though, he'd rest. He had less than a week until Christmas. Plenty of time.

"The Twelve Days of Christmas" lyrics chimed in his head as he drifted off. *On the twelfth day of Christmas, my mother abandoned me...*

The twelfth day would be here soon. And then he'd have eleven months until the blasted song and the holiday started tormenting him again.

He stretched out on the braided rug beside Carly and let her gentle breathing lull him to sleep.

With the storm bearing down on Tinley, he couldn't sleep long though.

An hour or two and he would be good to go.

He smiled as an image of his next victim flashed behind his eyes. Anticipation heated his blood.

The ornament would look lovely next to the holiday apron he'd picked out for her to wear.

CHAPTER EIGHT

3:15 A.M., December 19, Tinley

ALTHOUGH THE ONLY light coming from the motel was in the last room, Murphy eased along the front row, briefly pausing to listen at each door he passed in case someone was inside.

After all, even killers had to sleep.

He didn't detect any noise, so he continued toward the end of the row, staying close to the doorways to keep from being seen in case whoever was inside decided to look out.

As he grew closer, the sound of a male voice echoed from behind the closed door. He kept his gun at the ready and pressed himself flat against the wall by the window and listened. The curtains were drawn, preventing him from seeing who it was, but someone was definitely in there.

"It's all right," the voice murmured. "It'll be over soon."

Murphy froze as a woman's cry followed. Carly?

"Shh, we can't get caught now."

Anger tightened Murphy's muscles, and he debated on knocking, or charging into the room. But if the CK was

45

hurting Carly, he had to act quickly. The man could snap her neck in a second.

Bracing his gun, he balled his hand into a fist and knocked, then twisted the doorknob. The door was locked. He stepped back and kicked the thin wood. The door flew open, wood splintering.

"Police!" Except for the dim light in the bathroom, darkness bathed the room.

"What the hell?" a male voice shouted.

A female's shrill scream followed. Carly?

"Put your hands up where I can see them." He aimed his gun at the bed where the man stood and lifted his flashlight to illuminate the room.

Bright light glared across the paint-chipped walls and allowed him to see that the male was a teenager, not a man. "Don't shoot," the boy pleaded.

"No, don't shoot." The female started crying and snatching at the bedding to cover her nakedness.

Hell, he'd interrupted a teenage hook-up, not the CK and Carly.

The boy stood with his boxers around his ankles, hands raised in surrender, eyes wide with fear. "We ain't doin' nothing wrong," the boy stammered.

Murphy clenched his jaw. "You broke into this property," he growled. "What the hell are you two doing out here in the middle of the night? Don't you know we're in the middle of a blizzard?"

The girl yanked on a t-shirt, another sob escaping her, while the boy lifted his chin in a show of bravado meant to impress his girlfriend.

Dumb kid. She wouldn't be impressed if she wound up stranded out here with no heat or food for days.

"We just wanted some time alone," the boy said. "Her

parents freaked out the other night and said I can't come over no more."

The scent of weed wafted toward Murphy, and he gestured toward a joint on the end table. "I wonder why. You seem like such a responsible young man."

"I am," the boy blustered.

He ticked the boy's offenses off with his fingers, "You are in possession of an illegal substance. You are sleeping with an underage girl. And you could be charged with breaking and entering, plus statutory rape."

"I didn't rape her," the boy protested.

The girl looked up at him with tear-filled eyes. "We were just messing around."

"It's not like anyone uses this old place," the boy muttered.

"Shut up, the both of you," Murphy growled. "I should haul you to the station and keep you overnight just to teach you a damn lesson."

"Please don't." The girl trembled. "My daddy will kill me if I get arrested."

Murphy didn't know about that. He'd seen this girl around town. Her family was churchgoers. Not that attending church excluded the father from having a temper.

But he had more important things to do tonight than babysit them. He lowered his gun and stowed it in his holster. "All right. I'll let you off with a warning."

Wind whistled through the thin glass windows, and the girl shivered violently. The heat in the building had been turned off for years. He spotted the reflection of a candle flickering in the bathroom mirror.

"How did you get out here?" he asked.

"My truck," the boy answered. "I parked between some trees around back."

"Take the girl home," Murphy said. "Straight home, do

47

you hear me? Because if I learn you went somewhere else to finish this little rendezvous, I'll bring you both in. And no amount of pleading for mercy will stop me from pressing charges and calling your folks."

The teens exchanged terrified looks, and Murphy fought a smile. Throwing a little fear into them might keep them home safe where they belonged.

"One more thing," he said. "Did you see anyone else out here tonight?"

The two glanced back and forth confused. "It was just us," the boy said. "We didn't have a party if that's what you mean."

No, it wasn't. But he had his answer.

The teens hurriedly dressed then the girl grabbed the candle from the bathroom. The boy went for the weed, but Murphy shook his head. "Don't push it, kid."

A second later, the two pulled on their coats and ran toward the cluster of trees where they'd parked.

Murphy scowled. As a teenager, he'd done some stupid things. He'd snuck out with girls, too. But tonight, with the worst storm of the century marching through, their stupidity was just plain dangerous.

He closed up the room, then decided to check the other rooms just in case the CK had stowed Carly in one of them.

4:00 A.M., DECEMBER 19, TINLEY

A trilling sound roused Gia from unconsciousness. She opened her eyes, then blinked against the darkness.

Where was she? What the hell happened?

She rubbed her forehead and her hand came away with blood. She tasted it in her mouth, felt it trickling down the side of her cheek.

The blinding white outside hurt her eyes.

The car...she'd had an accident. On the way to Tinley to see the sheriff.

To find Carly.

And that noise...it was like a jackhammer to her skull.

Panic streaked through her.

Then she realized the sound was her phone.

Heart racing, she fumbled on the seat for her purse. Not on the seat.

In the floor where it had been tossed during the crash. The damn air bag was in the way. She wrestled with it and pushed it away enough to run her hand along the floorboard.

Her head throbbed as she dragged the purse back onto the seat. She wiped blood from her hand onto a tissue in her bag, then raked through the contents for her phone. Finally, her fingers connected with it at the bottom of the bag. The ringing stopped just as she snatched it and went to connect the call.

Gia released a shaky breath then checked the number, hoping it was the sheriff with good news. That he'd been wrong, and the Christmas Killer hadn't abducted Carly. When, in actuality, she was safe at the old homestead waiting on Gia to trim the live tree she'd brought home.

All wishful thinking of course.

Tears and panic blended, and she fought a scream and squinted to see the name on the screen.

Not the sheriff. Her partner had left a message.

"Gia, it's Brantley. Sorry, but I can't get out of the city. As of an hour ago, they've cancelled all flights going anywhere near the Midwest."

He sounded so upset that her chest squeezed with emotions. They'd only been working together for a few months, but he wanted to catch this serial killer as much as she did.

49

Yet now, as a gust of wind beat at the car, and she looked through the blinding snowstorm, she knew she was on her own. She quickly punched Brantley's number. When he answered, he sounded winded as if he was pacing back and forth.

"I got your message, and I understand," she said. "I barely made it on that last flight and there were hundreds of people stranded. I'm on my way to the sheriff's office now." She didn't bother to mention that she was sitting in a ditch.

"I'm so sorry, Gia. As soon as I can book a flight, I'll fly out there."

"It's all right," she said adopting her professional tone. "I'll call you when I know something."

Another wind torrent hurled a branch from a nearby tree, and it crashed into the passenger window. She ducked to avoid the spray of glass.

Then she glanced at the road hoping for help from a passerby. The truck that had run her off the road hadn't bothered to stop. And anyone with any sense had stayed off the road tonight.

With the temperature dropping, she had to call for help.

Now. If she was forced to spend the night in the car, she'd freeze to death. Then she'd be no good to her sister.

Shivering, she called Murphy's number. As she waited, she looked out at the falling snow and remembered a time when she and Carly had built a snowman on Christmas day then skated on the ice on the pond behind their house.

Their mother had been worried the ice would crack and they'd fall in. She felt as if she was skating on that ice now.

But it was thin and cracking, and Carly had already fallen in, and Gia couldn't reach her.

4:15 A.M., DECEMBER 19, TINLEY

Murphy's phone jangled as he finished searching the last motel room. It was empty.

Relief filled him that he hadn't found Carly dead inside, but worry gnawed at him. Where was she?

The clock was ticking.

His phone rang again, and he checked the number. He inhaled a deep breath and connected the call. "Gia?"

"Did you find Carly?"

His stomach clenched. "No, not yet. I searched the old motel outside of town, but she wasn't there. My deputy has a team combing every place we can think of. Where are you?"

"Here, well, almost to Tinley." She sounded shaken. Breathless. "I had an accident."

Dear God. "What? Are you all right?" Heart thudding in his chest, he tugged his coat up around his neck to ward off the worst of the wind.

He should have picked up her at the airport. She shouldn't be out there alone. She had to be all right.

A tense second passed.

"Gia?"

"I'm okay. But a truck came out of nowhere and crossed the centerline, and I lost control. I'm in a ditch about five miles from town."

He scrubbed a hand over his beard stubble, an image of Gia stranded in a ditch with snow piling up around her taunting him. "I'll call a tow truck, and I'll be there as soon I can."

He cursed as he tromped through the freshly falling snow and ice to his vehicle. Even with four-wheel drive, it would take him a few minutes to reach her.

She had sounded all right, hadn't she?

Of course, knowing Gia the way he did, she wouldn't

admit it if she was hurt.

He crawled in his vehicle and fired up the engine. The wipers screeched as they scraped the ice crystals on the glass. Heat blasted him as he pulled back onto the road, but all he could think about was Gia and whether or not she was lying.

She'd always been tough. Had broken her arm in a high school soccer tournament when she'd been tackled as she'd scored the winning goal for the championship game. But she hadn't told anyone, not until after the team left the field and the coach noticed her holding it close to her side.

She was too worried about her sister now to admit if she was injured.

But dammit, someone needed to take care of Gia. Whether she liked it or not, he'd damn well make himself that someone.

4:20 P.M., DECEMBER 19, TINLEY

Gia shivered and burrowed deeper into her coat. The wind outside tossed debris across the ground, the snow swirling in a white fog, frost forming icicles along the car window.

The clock mocked her from the dash. It had already been hours since her sister had called. Where was she now?

Had the Christmas Killer hurt her?

God help her. She'd been tracking this maniac for three weeks now and was no closer to learning his identity than she had been when the first body had been found on a dock on the Intracoastal Waterway in Delray.

The image of the woman's colorless face, ghostlike in death, taunted her. She'd been posed on a park bench facing the water wearing a red wool scarf, the ornament tied to her wrist, as if she was looking out at sea to watch the boats pass.

A local fisherman had found her when he'd been walking to his canoe at dawn. The young woman had been dead for hours. But the walkway bordering the Intracoastal was busy at night with locals and tourists, so the killer had to have slain her somewhere else and then brought her there when the area was deserted to pose her.

Rubbing her hands over her arms to warm herself, she retrieved the folder from her computer bag, opened it and spread the photographs of the other victims across the seat.

The victim profile was all over the place. Various body types, economic backgrounds, careers, and living quarters. They'd cross referenced every facet of the women's lives they could think of searching for a connection, from the restaurants they frequented to areas they shopped for food and clothing, churches they attended, social media contacts, clubs and gyms they belonged to—virtually dissecting the woman's lives apart detail by detail to determine a common denominator.

Three women had joined online dating sites, but none of the others had. Four had shared Facebook friendships, but nothing on their pages or the information the FBI had uncovered about the IP addresses offered a lead.

It was as if the sicko was picking his victims randomly from the crowd, which made it even more difficult to pinpoint who his next target would be.

Except Carly hadn't been a random choice. He'd made it personal because of her.

A sharp pang seized Gia as an image of her sister's face flashed behind her eyes. Carly posed somewhere in this den of ice and snow with a red ribbon encircling her slender wrist holding a damn ornament.

Carly out here in this godforsaken barren, flat ice land crying out for help and hoping Gia could save her...

CHAPTER NINE

5:00 A.M., December 19, Tinley

THE TIRES on Murphy's SUV churned ice and snow as he drove to meet Gia. He spotted her rental car in the ditch and pulled over onto the shoulder of the road.

Murphy cut the engine, climbed out and walked over to the vehicle. The engine was off, the snow coating the car in a two-inch layer. Another few hours and it might be buried.

His boots crunched ice and snow as he climbed into the ditch. He pressed one hand to the side of the car to maintain his footing as he moved to the driver's door and rapped on the window.

Through the frosted glass, Gia looked up at him, the strain on her face evident. He opened the car door and was instantly struck by how exhausted she looked. And how beautiful.

He'd thought the feelings he'd had for her in school would fade over time. He'd dated half a dozen women since. But every damn one of them he compared to Gia. And they'd come up lacking.

Not because they weren't nice ladies. Because they weren't *her*.

And now she was in crisis mode.

"Hi, Gia. I got here as fast as I could."

Relief spilled through her sigh. "Thanks for coming."

He noticed blood dotting her forehead. "Dammit, you are hurt." So like Gia to have to be the tough one.

She dabbed at the cut with her fingers, wiping blood away. "It's nothing."

"I'll drive you to the ER," Murphy said.

"No, I said I'm fine." Gia shot him a warning look. "I don't have time. The CK could be doing God knows what to Carly."

He ground his molars to keep from saying he would save the day. Be her hero. But what if he failed?

An engine sounded, and Ernie's Tow Truck service pulled up behind his SUV. Thankfully at this hour, Ernie had been home and hadn't been needed elsewhere. If people didn't heed the winter advisory and stay indoors the next couple of days, he'd be slammed with business.

"Thanks for coming," she said as she reached for her bag.

"No problem." He'd do anything for her. Maybe she didn't know it?

He glanced past her and saw crime photos spread across the seat of her car. Even stranded in a ditch, she was working.

"Let me get my things." She quickly gathered the pictures and stuffed them into a folder, then stored them in a large leather shoulder bag.

"Where's your suitcase?"

"The trunk," Gia said. "I'll get it."

He held up a hand. "I'll do it. Just pop the trunk."

She did as he said, and he helped her from the vehicle.

One look, and he realized she hadn't come prepared for the weather here in Nebraska. Her flat dress shoes sank into the snow, and her thin coat was made for much milder climates. The freezing temperatures had to be especially tough on her compared to South Florida.

She shivered, indicating she knew she was underdressed. Then again, she obviously hadn't been thinking about her wardrobe when she'd received that terrifying call.

He helped her maneuver her way to the back of the vehicle, and he retrieved her rolling bag from the trunk. Maybe she had more appropriate winter attire inside. The bitter swirled snow around them, the hazy fog of white nearly blinding as they climbed from the ditch.

Ernie was waiting, his face barely visible behind his full-face winter ski cap.

Murphy paused to introduce them, and Gia handed the man the keys to the rental. "Let me know about the repairs."

"Yes, Ma'am," Ernie said.

Gia thanked him, and Murphy placed his hand to the small of her back to steady her as they battled their way back to his SUV. He opened the passenger door and the force of the wind gusts practically pushed her inside.

Murphy stored her suitcase in the back of the SUV, then hurried to the driver's side. Once in the vehicle, he used his handkerchief to gently blot the blood from her forehead and see how deep the cut was.

She shrugged off his concern. "It's just a scratch. I want to go to the shop where Carly was abducted."

Murphy gritted his teeth and started the engine. He didn't blame her. But a protective streak surged through him. Seeing the shattered ornaments and her sister's blood wasn't going to be easy. He wanted to shield her from the truth.

Still, she knew more about this serial killer than anyone. If they were going to find him and her sister, they had to work together.

5:25 A.M., DECEMBER 19, TINLEY

Gia had forgotten how desolate the endless acres of farmland looked in the dead of winter. Her mother had thrived on living in the small town. She loved her neighbors and customers and volunteered for every church bake sale and charity the small town catered to.

She also organized toy drives in December for low-income kids as well as for the children's hospital and accompanied Santa Claus to hand out presents to the sick children.

Carly had assumed that role now.

And now she was missing. All because of *her*.

"I appreciate your help, Murph," she said, struggling to contain her rising panic.

"I'm sheriff now, Gia. It's my job," he said in a deep voice. His Midwestern accent wasn't quite as strong as she'd remembered. He'd filled out, put on muscle. His jaw was wide and strong, and covered with dark beard stubble. His thick black hair just long enough for a girl to run her fingers through it.

No wonder Carly had talked about him being handsome. He should be on a poster for cowboys, not in a sheriff's uniform.

Oblivious to her roving thoughts, he maneuvered the icy road. At this time of the morning, the streets were empty, and Tinley looked like a ghost town coated in a sea of endless white. Icicles dangled and clung to the store awnings like jagged knives, and the brutal wind whipped tree limbs and branches as if it might rip the trees from the ground.

"I know you're worried," Murphy said gently. "But we'll find her, Gia."

Emotions welled in her throat, but she swallowed, determined not to fall apart.

"I can't believe this is happening," she murmured.

"When did you last talk to her?" Murphy asked.

"Right after that press conference in Gulf Shores. She ... wanted me to come home for the holidays."

"Did she mention a friend or boyfriend she was close to?"

Gia startled as a tree limb snapped off and flew into the road. She hated to admit she hadn't known whether her sister had a boyfriend or not. "Not really. We just talked about Christmas and..." *You let her down again.*

Forget your pride. This is Carly's life and she's depending on you.

"And what?" Murphy probed.

"That's it," she said quietly. "I've been caught up in this case and traveling so much that I told her I wasn't coming." Regret seized her like a fist twisting her gut.

Now she might never see her sister again.

Hysteria balled in her throat, and she had to swallow twice to tamp it down.

Murphy's question about a potential boyfriend registered again, and the hair on the nape of her neck prickled. Was there a man in Carly's life? Someone new? "Do you know if she was seeing anyone?"

"I'm not sure. I saw her around town a couple of times talking to this veterinarian who was moving to Tinley."

Murphy steered the vehicle around a curve and passed the welcome sign to Tinley which was flapping wildly in the wind. Christmas garland wound around the pole holding the sign and was tangled now and torn. Beside it, a giant metal elf pointed toward the town square where the festival was usually held.

"What? Who is he?"

"Name's Dr. Parker Whitman. He visited town at the beginning of the month, scouting out space to open a vet clinic."

"Is he still here?" she asked.

"I called him, but he was headed out of town to visit family for the holidays."

A frisson of alarm traipsed up Gia's spine. "Can you verify he's really with family?"

A frown creased Murphy's broad forehead. "I haven't. But I will."

Suspicions mounted in her mind. The timing of the man's appearance in Tinley might be important.

What if this vet was the Christmas Killer?

The perp committed his first kill on December 1st. He waited a day or two in between victims. She'd been assigned the case from the beginning and had addressed the public after the third murder, when they'd determined they were dealing with a serial killer.

The Christmas Killer was methodical. He planned out his crimes. The profile indicated he was charming.

A possible scenario formed in her mind. He could have flown to Tinley following her first press conference regarding the first CK victim. Then he started a charade about opening a clinic here because he'd researched her and knew her sister lived here.

Then he'd met Carly and pretended to be her friend.

"Did this Whitman guy buy or rent a place in Tinley when he was here?"

Murphy swung his SUV in front of *Happy Holidays*! and parked, then turned to look at her. "I think he stayed at the motel. But I can check with Tamika at Tinley Realty and find out."

"Do that," Gia said. "We have to consider every possibility. Let's make sure this guy is who he claims to be, that he didn't disguise himself as a vet to win Carly's trust so he could abduct her without being noticed."

She didn't bother to wait on a response. She shoved open the door and climbed out of the car. Her feet sank into the freezing snow and the wind battered her, nearly knocking her over. Murphy grabbed her arm to steady her, and she breathed out a sigh. Even though he was simply helping her, his touch reminded her how much she'd liked him years ago. How much she'd missed him.

How long it had been since she'd let any man get close to her.

You don't have time to think about what could have been.

Besides, Murphy had put a red light on their dating. He'd been brooding. Angry. She'd heard rumors his old man had been mean to him, but he hadn't wanted to talk about it.

Focus on Carly.

Straightening, she pulled away and plodded her way up the sidewalk to the entrance to Carly's store.

The yellow crime scene tape flapping in the blustery wind looked stark against the red and green tinsel stringing from the door to *Happy Holidays!*

Images of her mother and sister greeting customers with hot chocolate and cookies as they entered nearly brought her to her knees as she ducked beneath the crime tape for Murphy to let her inside.

5:30 A.M., DECEMBER 19, TINLEY

Murphy opened the door for Gia, his mind racing as he contemplated her statement about Dr. Parker Whitman.

What if she was right and Whitman wasn't who he claimed to be?

Living in Tinley had allowed Murphy to breathe. To drop his defenses. To finally forget about what a jerk his old man was and to believe in the good side of people.

What if he'd made a mistake in letting down his guard?

He was the sheriff, supposed to protect innocents.

It hadn't occurred to him before that Whitman would have lied about who he was. The guy seemed friendly, kind, even tempered. He opened the door for the ladies in town and had seemed polite and easy going.

But...he hadn't stayed in town for more than a couple of days at a time. And his visits had started three weeks ago. About the same time Gia had been seen on TV announcing a serial killer was stalking the South.

Like the rest of the nation, Murphy had been angry and shocked that a man would prey on women. Doing so at the holidays made the crimes even more heinous. But the killer had struck hundreds of miles from his home. The citizens of Tinley had been safe.

Or so he thought.

Gia's sharp intake of breath jerked him back to the moment. She stood a foot away from the Christmas tree. Not wanting to contaminate the scene, she stayed clear of the blood, broken ornaments glass and packages. "This is where it happened," she said in a raw whisper.

Grim-faced, Murphy nodded. "It looks like they struggled. She probably tried to grab the tree to steady herself or maybe to swing it at him so she could run. Some of the ornaments fell off in the struggle." He pointed to the crimson stains on the floor. "She may have cut herself on the ornaments, and that's her blood."

"Or he cut himself and it's his." Hope tinged her voice.

"The crime team took samples and processed the shop, including the walls, doors and doorknobs. They found a tiny button on the floor by the singing snowman. Don't know if it belonged to a customer or to him, but we bagged it. Forensics should be at the lab now. I asked them to put a rush on it so maybe we'll know in a few hours."

A tense pause, then Gia offered him a tiny smile. "Thanks for being so thorough, Murphy."

"I may be small town, Gia, but I do my job. This maniac walked into my town and abducted one of our own," he said. "I want to get Carly back safely and stop him before he hurts anyone else." And with tourists already in Tinley, the victim pool was growing larger.

Having strangers around would also enable the killer to hide without attracting attention.

Gia averted her eyes, although he detected tears threatening. Seeing her vulnerable and frightened roused every instinct he had to draw her into his arms and comfort her. But she'd pulled away when he'd taken her arm outside, so he kept his hands to himself.

She angled her head toward him. "Where's the ornament?"

Murphy gestured toward the register. "I found it tied to the little tree Carly kept on top of the counter. But I had the crime team bag it all and send to the lab."

"It's odd he left it there," she mused. "He usually ties it to the victim's wrist."

"Maybe it's a sign he hasn't hurt her yet," Murphy said. "Or that we're dealing with a

copycat. You didn't release that detail to the press, did you?"

Gia shook her head. "No, but I don't think it's a copycat." She tucked an errant strand of hair that had escaped her ponytail behind one ear. "It feels like it's him. Like he came here to torment me." A myriad of emotions streaked her face. "I think he wants me now. That he kidnapped Carly to torment me because I'm his end game."

CHAPTER TEN

5:45 A.M., December 19, Tinley

THE SCENT of apple turnovers and chocolate croissants made him dizzy as he thought of his mother. Every year at holiday time, she'd bake cinnamon rolls and gingerbread men. Together, they'd decorate sugar cookies with icing and sprinkles, then sip hot chocolate while they watched old Christmas movies.

The twinkling colored lights had mesmerized him. Then they'd cut out paper snowflakes and strung them all around the house.

His daddy had hated it though. He'd come home smelling like whiskey and cheap perfume, and he'd yelled at his mother to take down the gaudy looking decorations. Said the blow-up Santa and elf in the yard looked like white trash.

She'd argued with him once, said they were pretty, but he'd shoved her down and told her nothing was pretty about her or the stupid Christmas tree. Then his father had seen the Twelve Days ornaments and begun crushing them.

"Stop it, Daddy!" He lunged at his father and tried to grab the ornaments to save them. They were special between him and his mother.

But his father backhanded him so hard he went flying across the room. He hit the wall with a thud, tasted blood, and his nose had gushed.

His mother cried out for him to run to his room and stay there. That night as he lay huddled in bed, too afraid to come out, his parents had screamed and fought. He'd heard the lamp crash and tables being overturned and things smashing against the wall.

Finally, he'd cried himself to sleep. When he'd woken up in the morning and gotten up the courage to come out, all the decorations had been destroyed and thrown in the garbage.

His mother was gone, too.

She'd abandoned him and left him with that monster. After that, he'd hated Christmas and any reminder of the stupid holiday.

But he couldn't escape the glitter and sparkles this time of year. It was everywhere.

This town was worse than some others.

He'd heard the disappointed whispers of the locals as they talked about having to cancel the parade and the festival. The blizzard was wreaking havoc on their yearly traditions.

Still, the girl in the sweet shop had been friendly to him and insisted the festival would go on, that the town wouldn't let it die. It would just start a couple of days later.

As if he cared.

Yes, Sweet Sari had offered him free samples and smiled at him like she enjoyed waiting on him.

Just like a woman should.

Not all of the girls did. Some were snooty and aloof and acted as if he was nobody.

That was their mistake.

Still, he had to take her. She would make a perfect number ten.

He stood beneath the thick trees bordering her driveway and waited on her. He'd heard her say she usually left for work by four a.m. But today, with the storm in full swing, she planned to wait until daylight. The bakery would be closed for the day.

But she had food to deliver to the search teams looking for Carly.

Laughter bubbled in his chest, and he dug his hands into his pockets and ground his teeth to keep them from chattering.

Those workers would just have to do without her homemade goodies.

He had other plans for Sari.

CHAPTER ELEVEN

6:00 A.M., December 19, Tinley

THE SIGHT of the shattered angel ornament on the floor twisted at the last vestiges of Gia's composure.

But she channeled her energy into professional mode and mentally distanced herself from the reality that violence now tainted *Happy Holidays*! If she didn't, she'd virtually collapse into a puddle of tears.

Although Murphy and the crime scene team had photographed the shop, she wanted her own pictures. Often, she noticed things long after her initial assessment. Usually late at night when she should be sleeping but was too wired to close her eyes.

She didn't have time for sleep now. Every second counted.

Judging from the broken ornaments, crushed packages and gnarled tree limbs, she agreed with Murphy's theory. However, the ornaments on the countertop tree stumped her slightly.

He'd obviously wanted her to think he was the Christmas

Killer, but could he be a copycat? She didn't see how that was possible, unless someone had leaked the details of his MO to the press?

Or...as she'd thought earlier...was he holding Carly just to torment her? If so, that meant he would take another woman.

Probably within the next few hours.

She crossed the room to the counter. With gloved hands, she examined the box of opened ornaments. On the bottom of the box, she saw the *Happy Holidays!* price tag sticker.

"He has his own set of ornaments," she told Murphy as she dove into the killer's mind. "This box came from the store. That's the reason he left the last three ornaments here. The tenth ornament on the tree is a warning that he's hunting his tenth victim."

"He's playing cat and mouse," he said darkly. "I don't want to panic folks, but we have to warn the women in town."

Worry knotted Gia's insides. "You're right."

"The residents are already upset about the storm hindering the festival. And now this." Murphy scrubbed his hand over his face. "Do you have any idea who he might target?"

Gia bit down on her bottom lip. "So far, he appears to be choosing his victims at random."

"Would you mind showing me those crime scene photos? Maybe a pair of fresh eyes could help."

"True. God knows I've looked at them a hundred times. And so has my partner. We have another agent analyzing them as well."

"We could do it at my office."

Gia agreed, then photographed the box of ornaments. Murphy led her toward the back, and they followed the blood trail to the rear door. She looked inside the storage closets, but they were overflowing.

She'd practically lived in the store growing up and had

worked as a salesclerk during the holiday rush. Since then, Carly had reorganized inventory to make it easy to locate specific products. Gia combed the shelves and eventually found the one holding specialty ornaments. Four boxes of the Twelve Days of Christmas ornaments were stacked on top. She pointed them out to Murphy.

"Did your people fingerprint inside the closet?" she asked.

Murphy shook his head. "I don't think so. But I'll grab my kit from the car and do it now."

"Thanks." While he hurried to his vehicle, she snapped pictures of the blood trail. Not enough blood to indicate that Carly had been seriously injured.

But enough to indicate that the sheriff was right. Carly had struggled during the abduction.

"Hang in there, sis, and keep fighting. I'm going to find you," she whispered.

From her vantage on the floor, she spotted something beneath the corner of the door leading to Carly's office. She leaned over and peered at it, then realized it was a business card.

The card was from a pet grooming shop in Gulf Shores. The shop owned by victim number nine.

A second later, the lights flickered off, pitching the store into full darkness.

Footsteps sounded on the wooden floor. "Murphy?"

No response.

She jerked her head up, hand on her weapon, ready in case the killer had come back here for her.

6:10 A.M., DECEMBER 19, TINLEY

As Murphy headed back into the store, he couldn't shake the realization that the CK might have already chosen another woman in Tinley as his next victim.

Just as he entered, the lights went off.

Hell. Holly was definitely gaining momentum. Outside, snow fell in heavy thick flakes and the wind stirred it from the ground and trees, swirling it in a blinding haze.

He pulled his flashlight and flicked it on, then hurried toward the back of the store. "Gia?"

Breathing echoed in the silence, and he paused, listening. Had someone snuck inside while he went to his car?

Every instinct in him jumped to attention, and he eased his way toward the closet where he'd left Gia. He scanned the front of the shop, the tree, and behind the register counter. Nothing.

The floor squeaked beneath his boots. "Gia?"

A noise echoed from near the closet, then her voice. "I'm here."

He shined his flashlight across the hallway then found her standing behind the closet door, her gun in her hand.

"Whoa." He lifted his own weapon in surrender, then gestured for them to both put their weapons away.

"The lights went off, and I thought he might have gotten in," she whispered in a shaky voice.

"Same here," he said gruffly as he holstered his weapon. "You okay?"

She nodded, although she seemed anything but okay. She looked fatigued and out of her mind with worry.

She had every right to be.

She held out her hand. "I found this business card on the floor wedged beneath the door."

Murphy took a step closer. Her fingers trembled as she

handed the card to him. "The name of that pet grooming service is the same one owned by victim nine, Terry Ann Igley."

He arched a brow. "You think he intentionally left it so you'd know he's here?"

Her eyes narrowed in thought. "I don't think so. If he had, he would have left it in plain sight, on the register counter."

"Then he may have touched it without gloves. I'll send it to the lab ASAP."

He stowed it in an evidence bag, then stepped into the storage closet. "Let me dust this place, then we'll get out of here."

The lights suddenly flickered back on, casting them in bright light. "I'll look at that blood trail while you process the closet."

He gave a quick nod and decided to get to work before they completely lost power. It was only a matter of time before the entire town was in the dark.

Murphy found a partial print on the edge of the shelf. Although it could be Carly's or one of the teens she hired during the holiday rush to stock shelves and assist with customers, it might also belong to her kidnapper.

"I need to issue a warning and alert people as to the situation," Murphy reiterated. "How about we grab breakfast and coffee? Then we'll stop by my office and look at those crime scene photos."

6:30 A.M., DECEMBER 19, TINLEY

Bubba's Breakfast and Grille had become a landmark for Tinley residents to gather over late morning stacks of hotcakes, sausage, bacon, ham and buttermilk biscuits.

Lunches ranged from salads and homemade soups to desserts provided by Sari's Sweetshop. It also attracted tourists with a penchant for burgers and beer.

Bubba's wife baked hotdishes, "casseroles" as Gia had learned they called them in the South, and during corn harvest season, they offered twenty varieties of corn ranging from street corn to creamed sweet corn and included special seasoning and rubs that spiced up the local fanfare. Corn and bean salsa was a mainstay for Bubba's and proved to be the perfect side dishes for Bubba's breakfast burritos.

Just like the rest of the town, holiday decorations adorned the establishment. Someone had painted snowflakes on the windows, ironic since now real snow clung to the glass and icicles hung from the awnings.

Jingle bells tinkled as Murphy opened the door and "Silent Night" flowed from the speakers as Gia headed toward a booth. A giant Santa sitting beside the old-fashioned jukebox waved in greeting and hand carved wooden reindeer lined the breakfast bar counter.

Exhaustion clawed at Gia's muscles as she sank into a booth. Green and red tablecloths covered the tables, while mason jars filled with sprigs of holly added to the festive environment.

Today they made Gia feel even more depressed.

Her sister loved the season and all the color and cheer. Now she was in the clutches of a crazed killer.

Bubba's wife, Arlene, brought over a pot of coffee. "Gia Franklin, I declare, I didn't expect to see you ever come home. Carly talks about you all the time." She waved her hand dramatically. "Don't 'cha know! Gia's working this important case and Gia's flying here and there."

The thought of her sister bragging about her when Gia had dismissed her pleas to visit twisted the knife deeper into her heart.

Her emotions must have shown on her face because the older woman's eyes suddenly widened. "Oh, dear, what's wrong?"

Bubba lumbered over with a basket of homemade biscuits and honey. "Didn't you see that crime scene tape in front of *Happy Holidays!*, Arlene?"

Arlene's face paled, and she gripped the edge of the table as if her knees went weak. "Carly... where is she?"

Murphy cleared his throat. "That's the reason Gia is here," he said matter-of-factly. "Unfortunately, we don't know where Carly is at the moment. Someone abducted her from her store."

Arlene sank down onto the seat beside Gia. "Oh, my goodness, honey. Carly has to be all right."

"Yes, she has to be," Gia murmured, although her voice wavered.

Bubba, a big blustery thick-chested man with a scruffy beard, gave Gia a sympathetic look. But his take-charge voice was comforting. "How can we help?"

"I don't want to stir up panic," Murphy said. "But we have reason to believe the man Gia has been chasing for those multiple murders is here. That he kidnapped Carly to get back at Gia."

Arlene gasped, her age-spotted hand fluttering to her face. "You're talking about the Christmas Killer? The one who murdered all those young girls?"

Young ones just like her sister. Gia nodded, nausea climbing her throat. "I'm afraid so. I hopped on a plane and got here as soon as I could."

"My deputy is organizing search parties to hunt for her," Murphy said. "Bubba, we might need your help."

"I'll get in touch with all my friends, the men's church group, and my bowling team," Bubba offered. "They'll want to join the search."

"If that maniac is in Tinley, the young women around here are in danger," Arlene cried.

Gia shifted restlessly. Simply the mention of that serial killer's name would rouse panic in town. "I'm afraid so," she said. "I don't want to create hysteria, but we have to warn locals and tourists."

"I'm planning to talk to the local news station," Murphy said. "And I'll have them issue a press release."

The front door opened, and a gust of wind blew in as two families appeared, chattering about needing a hot breakfast. Bubba and Arlene's daughter Billy Jo hurried to show them to their tables. Gia hadn't seen her in three years. She'd matured into a pretty teenager.

"Already we've postponed the parade and festivities for today and tomorrow, but the town council was hoping we could salvage Christmas Eve and Christmas Day," Arlene said. "News of this will make people flee the town and not come back."

"Arlene," Bubba chided, his tone slightly sharp. "The last thing Gia is worried about now is the Christmas Festival. Her sister is missing."

Arlene's face crumpled. "Oh, I'm so sorry, dear. I didn't mean to sound like I don't care. I adore Carly. She's done so much for Tinley since your mother died. I swear, sometimes I walk into the store and I feel like your mama is still here with us."

Gia blinked back tears and took a long sip of her coffee, grateful for the burst of caffeine.

"I don't think people will be leaving in this weather," Murphy told Arlene. "If the storm intensifies like the weather forecasters are predicting, roads will be impassable. Airports are already shutting down."

The front door opened again, and other customers began to meander in.

Gia and Murphy both ordered the morning special, then Arlene hurried away.

Bubba's hand went to his cell phone. "I'll start making calls."

"Tell everyone to contact my deputy," Murphy said. "He's in charge of organizing the search parties, establishing search grids and assigning teams for each area."

Bubba gave a quick nod, then headed toward the kitchen, already punching in contacts on his cell phone.

Gia had once hated living in this small town where everyone knew everyone's business. But at the moment, she remembered how nice it was when someone was in trouble. Everyone pitched in to help however they could.

She and Murphy needed all the help they could get.

"I'll call our local news anchor." Murphy headed toward the hall leading to the men's room.

Gia checked her phone for messages. Nothing from Brantley or the killer. She called Brantley's number and sipped her coffee while she waited.

He answered a minute later. "Any news on your sister?"

Gia blotted up sweetener from the packet she'd spilled on the table. Anything to distract herself. "No. But I have a name I want you to check out. Dr. Parker Whitman."

"Who is he?"

"He came to Tinley a couple of weeks ago, right after we aired the story that we were dealing with a serial. Sheriff Malone says he met Carly when he was in town."

"Do you have a picture?"

"No, but I'll see if I can obtain one." She wound her pony-tail around her fingers. "Anyway, he claimed he was a vet and was looking for space to open a clinic. Sheriff called him to ask if he'd seen Carly, but he said he was headed out of town to visit family. I found a business card with a phone number, and the sheriff talked to him on a cell, but he's not answering now. I need you to find out everything and anything you can on the man."

"What makes you think he's our perp?" Brantley asked.

"I don't know if he is." Frustration edged her words. "But at the moment, we have to consider every possibility. The timing of his appearance in Tinley, his short visits, and now his disappearance seem too coincidental to ignore."

"I'm on it. Text me the numbers and I'll see what I can dig up. And if you find a photo, that would be the bomb."

"I'll see what I can do." Although if this man was the Christmas Killer, he most likely wouldn't have allowed himself to be caught on camera anywhere in town.

Not that the people in Tinley had security cameras anyway. They were all so trusting. She'd learned not to trust on the job a long time ago.

A violent wind burst practically shook the café. "Call or text me whether you find anything or not. And if you can't reach me, contact the local sheriff's office here. This blizzard is on top of us. We might lose power and cell service today."

"Will do. If you need anything else, just let me know."

"The only thing I need is to find Carly," Gia said, her voice a pained whisper.

He murmured that he understood and hung up, and Gia looked up to see more families entering the restaurant and grill. All were bundled up, some laughing about the impending storm, others grousing about the biting wind and how this wasn't their idea of spending Christmas in Tinsel Town.

Anger blended with panic and a helpless feeling that she hated more than anything. Struggling to control her emotions, she replayed the half dozen messages Carly had left her earlier in the week. Each time Carly had begged her to come home.

But she'd ignored them.

Guilt robbed her breath. If she'd been here, she could have prevented her sister from being taken. And tonight they'd be trimming the tree together instead of Carly fighting for her life.

Unless she was already dead.

CHAPTER TWELVE

WHEN MURPHY PHONED the local news station, he asked for Clarissa Klondike, the lead anchorwoman.

"Morning, Sheriff."

He wished he could say it was a good one. "Hi, Clarissa. We need to talk."

"You have five minutes," she said. Noise echoed in the background. Voices. People moving around. "The storm is speeding toward us, and I've got everyone on deck working to cover it."

"This is important, another big story," he said. "I need your help."

"Hang on, let me shut my door." A second later, the noise died down. "Okay, this sounds serious. What's up?"

"One of our residents, Carly Franklin, is missing."

A heartbeat of silence. "You think she had an accident? Or she's stranded somewhere? A few miles north of here, residents lost power and we just got word of a building collapsing. Rescue workers are on the scene now."

Ahh, geesh. "Let me know what they find. But this is about the Christmas Killer."

Clarissa released a long-winded sigh. "You think he's here in Tinley? That he has Carly?"

"I think so." Murphy explained about Gia's phone call from her sister and the killer's message. "He's making it personal."

"You're right, this is huge," Clarissa said. "Do you want me to run with the story?"

Murphy was torn. Going public would cause fear in locals and visitors. But he'd be remiss if he kept quiet. And they needed all eyes looking for this madman. "If he sticks to his schedule, he'll be hunting another victim. We have to warn residents and tourists, tell women not to travel or go out alone. To be hyper vigilante about taking safety precautions."

"In the midst of the blizzard, most people will be staying in," Clarissa said. "That could help."

"True. But it would be irresponsible not to inform the public. Post my office phone number and emphasize that if anyone sees or hears anything suspicious, they should call in." He drummed his fingers on the table. "Can you get this on the local TV and radio stations right away?"

"As soon as we hang up," Clarissa said.

"Thanks, Clarissa. I hate to incite panic. But it's better than losing another woman to this madman."

"Agreed." She hesitated. "You said Gia Franklin is in town?"

"Yes," Murphy said. "We're going to my office to review the details of the case. My deputy started organizing search parties as soon as she called last night. He'll be overseeing them all day today." His pulse hammered.

Of course, they might need manpower to help first responders if the blizzard proved as bad as predicted. Already lives
had been lost in Montana and Colorado. Downed power lines,
dangerous roads, and falling trees could also prove deadly.

"Sheriff, do you think Gia would want to go on camera
and make a statement?"

Murphy looked at Gia as he walked back to the table. "I'll
ask her." The strain of the night and exhaustion carved deep
grooves beside her eyes.

His heart gave a pang as he remembered the grief on her
face at her mother's funeral. Carly was the only family she
had left.

She'd be devastated if she lost her sister.

8:00 A.M., DECEMBER 19, TINLEY

Gia hated dealing with the press again, but if it meant saving
a life, she would do it.

She and Murphy met Clarissa Klondike at his office. By
the time the anchorwoman arrived, Clarissa had arranged for
a local crew to be present.

Nerves bunched in Gia's belly, and she wished she hadn't
eaten breakfast. But she needed fuel for energy. Today might
prove to be the longest day of her life.

The cameraman Eric Garrison greeted her and Murphy
with a solemn expression. "I've been keeping up with the
story about the Christmas Killer. I'm sorry to hear he has
your sister."

Gia swallowed hard in an effort not to break down. She
had to get through this. "He saw me on the news yesterday in
Gulf Shores. He took her because of me."

"We'll do whatever we can to help you find her and stop him," Eric assured her.

Clarissa cleared her throat. "The radio stations are already blasting precautions about the blizzard. As soon as we're finished here, we'll ask them to add a special segment focusing on the Christmas Killer and Carly's disappearance."

Murphy squared his shoulders and thanked her. 'Tinley residents have always jumped in to help one another. I have no doubt in my mind they will now."

The sheriff's confidence bolstered Gia's own. A blessing to live in a small town. People cared about each other and offered support when one of their own was in trouble.

She'd missed that. Missed the kind of strength being around Murphy offered.

Missed him.

"Are you ready, Special Agent Franklin?" Eric asked.

Gia inhaled a deep breath and nodded. Somehow, she had to find a way to get through to the sicko who had Carly. She just hoped he was watching.

8:15 A.M., DECEMBER 19, TINLEY

Murphy watched Gia address the public with a mixture of admiration and concern as she spoke about the case and her sister. She gave a gallant effort to keep her voice steady, but fear and worry tinged her tone.

She finished with a heartfelt plea. "People, we have already lost nine young women to this madman. Please help me stop him before he adds another name to his list."

Gia glanced his way and he stepped up to speak. "Carly Franklin has donated her time and money to gathering toys for needy children and for the children's hospital. Let's show her our love now. Here are ways you can help. Call my office and speak with my deputy about joining one of our search parties. Also, if you were near *Happy Holidays!* in the past forty-eight hours and saw anything suspicious, please contact the sheriff's office right away." He paused. "And last but not least, ladies, be careful. Travel together. As much as we love welcoming strangers to our town, this is a time to be cautious. The blizzard that has already barreled across two states is upon us, so my advice is to stay home with your families or friends."

He cited the phone number for his office and ended with the tip line number the FBI had set up.

"We'll get this across radio and TV stations immediately," Clarissa told him.

She and Eric packed up their equipment, and Murphy walked them outside. The sky was dark, snow clouds hanging heavy and barely visible with the precipitation increasing. The wind tossed twigs and debris across the street, tearing the Christmas garland from the streetlamps and store awnings and whipping it through the air. A shudder flapped on the Sari's Sweets bakery across the street and the force of the wind blew the fake Santas and elves in front of *Happy Holidays!* to the sidewalk.

Clarissa and Eric raced through the foot-deep snow as fast as they could, battling the wind gusts and blinding snowfall. Patrons at Bubba's were dashing out to their cars or walking to the inn, hopefully to stay tucked inside for the day.

He tugged his jacket up around his neck as he surveyed the street front. The maniac who'd abducted Carly had escaped nine times. How in the hell would they find him—and Carly—in this frigid mess?

8:20 A.M., DECEMBER 19, TINLEY

Gia found Murphy's whiteboard and marker and spread her files on the table beside it. Next she listed all the information she'd gleaned on the Christmas Killer.

She'd studied the victims so much that she'd memorized the victims' names and intricate details about their lives. Her team had done the same, all searching for a method to this killer's madness.

Murphy strode in, carrying two cups of coffee. He set one on the table for her, and she murmured thanks then gestured toward the photos and information she'd tacked on the board.

"The first three victims all lived in Delray Beach, Florida," she said as she began sharing details about the case with Murphy.

"Victim one—Page Gleeson, twenty-seven-years old, single, a coffee barista at a coffee shop a block from the boardwalk at Delray Beach. According to her coworkers, she left the coffee shop after her shift ended at nine and was walking home. She never made it. Police canvassed the area, but it was a busy night, and no one noticed Page or what happened to her. Body was found in the coffee shop at four a.m. the next morning by a coworker when he opened up.

"Victim two—Kittie Preston, twenty-four, engaged to a grad student. He was questioned and had a rock-solid alibi. She worked at a shoe store at the mall where she was last seen leaving around ten o'clock p.m. Her car was left in the parking lot where we believe she was taken." Gia paused to put the grisly images of the victims out of her head. "Police reviewed security cameras but the two on the south end weren't working, so found nothing. Body was discovered on the beach by an early morning jogger. She was wearing a pair of red heels and an ugly Christmas sweater."

Murphy sat quietly, absorbing the details. His solid presence had a calming effect on Gia, made it easier to talk about previous victims of the man who had her sister.

"Victim three—Anita Henderson, twenty-five, single, owned a food truck that catered to local events. She was last seen at a music festival, which drew hundreds of people. It appears he abducted her during one of the concerts, but again no witnesses. Body discovered in her own food truck the next morning. She was propped against the serving counter as if waiting on a customer wearing a Santa cap.

"The next three victims were found in Savannah, Georgia." Gia paused to take a fortifying sip of coffee.

"Victim four—Avery Wong, twenty-one, single, on vacation with her girlfriends. According to her friends, they went shopping at the tourist's shops on River Street, then had drinks at a bar. Avery complained of a migraine and left early to walk back to the hotel. When the girls got back, Avery wasn't there. Her body was discovered by the hotel pool at five a.m. in a red and green striped bathing suit when some guests, returning from partying all night, decided to skinny dip.

"Victim five—Lucy Crandall, twenty-two, worked at a t-shirt/souvenir shop by the river. Single, working her way through college. She was last seen going for a run from her apartment. No clues or suspects. Body was found in the park on a bench wearing a souvenir Christmas shirt and jogging shorts."

Images of her own sister, surrounded by the trappings of a holiday she loved, brought a lump to Gia's throat. She cleared it, brought herself under control and continued the grisly briefing.

"Victim six—Ruthie Pickley, twenty-eight, a waitress at the Crab Hut, last seen leaving for a date. She met the guy on-line, but we tracked him down and he claims he went to meet her, but she never showed. Witnesses confirm he was at the restaurant where they were supposed to meet, that he called his buddy who met him there for drinks when Ruthie stood him up. She was found in a holiday waitress uniform in a gazebo by the pier holding a bucket of crabs."

Images of her sister's blood-spattered shop almost undid Gia.

"Now the perp moved onto Gulf Shores." The staggering number of victims had her reaching for her cup again, taking courage from the small burst of caffeine.

"Victim seven—Sissy Wiggins, cleaned rooms at the Motel Five. Last seen leaving the night before to attend a yoga class which she never made. Again, police checked cameras at the hotel, questioned her coworkers, and investigated everyone on the guest registry. Nothing. Body discovered below the yoga sign in front of the gym, dressed in yoga pants and a Christmas tank.

"Victim eight—Marcia Sanchez, twenty-nine, engaged to a soldier who is currently deployed. She worked at a donut shop on the strip by the beach. Cameras inside the shop show her chatting with customers throughout the morning, but none of them fit the profile of the killer. She was found at the drive-through counter with holiday donuts stacked in front of her.

Gia wouldn't think about Carly's love for the holidays right now. *Couldn't* think of it.

Murphy shifted uncomfortably. "This guy is beyond sick."

Gia nodded and went on. "Victim nine—Terry Ann Igley, had a live-in girlfriend. Vic owned a pet grooming and boarding service that catered to tourists. Body was found in one of her dog cages with a sign encouraging people to give rescue puppies as Christmas gifts."

Murphy made a disgusted sound. "He's really making a mockery out of the holiday."

Gia nodded. "We don't know why yet, but that's true."

Murphy ran a hand through his thick hair. "He doesn't seem to have a type. Some are blondes, others are brunettes, and some are redheads."

"Exactly. "Gia sighed, her gaze skating over the photographs again. She hadn't been able to bring herself to add Carly's photo.

"The only commonality between the girls is the fact that they all work in service industry jobs where they meet a multitude of people during the day."

"That's how he meets them, so he doesn't stand out. And they're forced to interact with them."

"True. He may misinterpret their reaction to him as personal interest, or rejection," Gia suggested.

Murphy frowned. "The fact that he's moving from state to state is unusual, isn't it?"

"Not that unusual. He may be hopping from one place to another to mess with us, and of course, to avoid being caught. He probably likes watching us run around trying to figure out where he'll go next. That gives him time to travel to his next location and stake out his next victim."

Murphy nodded. "Wasn't there a case where a man murdered women along the interstate?"

Her stomach knotted. "You're right, there was."

"What if there's more to it than random moving from one state to the other? What if these states mean something to him?"

Gia's mind raced. "That's possible. The first three are all Southern states. But then he came all the way here to Nebraska." Emotions caught in her throat. "Of course, that was because of me."

Murphy's dark eyes locked with hers. "Maybe. But think about it. His traveling could have something to do with his job. What if he's a traveling salesman or a trucker? He's used to being on the road and encountering the type of service people you described."

Gia's pulse jumped. So far, they had a working profile, but they hadn't narrowed down a career for the man.

If Murphy was right, and his theory *did* make sense, maybe their analyst at the bureau could find a suspect who fit the profile and give them a viable suspect.

8:35 A.M., DECEMBER 19, TINLEY

Murphy's phone buzzed on his hip. He snagged it, every muscle in his body tight with apprehension. Seeing all those young women's names on one board and looking at their innocent faces roused a deep-seated rage.

He wanted to find this monster and make him pay.

His phone buzzed again, and he connected while Gia called the Bureau. Earlier, he'd left a message at the real estate agency.

"Hello, Sheriff, it's Lea Gomez from Tinley Realty. You left a message for Tamika?"

"Yes."

"She texted saying to close the agency today because of the storm," Lea said. "Is there something I can do for you?"

"I hope so. Did you see the news story about Carly Franklin's disappearance?"

"Yes, that's awful. I really liked her. My church group started a prayer chain as soon as we heard. Have you found her yet?"

"I'm afraid not," he answered. "I'm talking to everyone or anyone who knew her. I saw her with that veterinarian Parker Whitman around town. What do you know about him?"

"Not that much," Lea said. "Tamika said he was nice.

Why? Do you think he had something to do with her disappearance?"

"I don't know, I'm just asking questions right now. Tamika showed him some property, didn't she?"

"I believe she did. A couple of places. One was an abandoned warehouse off First Street she thought he might be able to convert to a vet clinic."

Murphy clenched his jaw. An abandoned warehouse would be the perfect place to hold a hostage. "Did he look at any other property to buy or rent for a home?" Murphy asked.

"Hmm, let me check. I believe Tamika keeps a log of places she shows."

A clicking sound, computer keys tapping on the keyboard, echoed in the background. A minute later, Lea returned. "Actually, she did show Dr. Whitman some additional properties. A cottage at Cottages by the Creek, but that sold before he could put in an offer. Then a rental farmhouse on Old Mill Road. Tamika made a note indicating he liked that one."

Murphy sucked in a sharp breath. The Franklin house was off of Old Mill Road.

He'd check out the abandoned warehouse then head over there.

"How else can I help?" the realtor asked.

"You could do me a favor. Call the owner of Cottages by the Creek and Mistletoe Inn and get a copy of their guest lists. If they're worried about protecting their guests' privacy, tell them I requested this and explain the reason."

"Of course. I'll fax the lists over as soon as I receive them."

Murphy thanked her and ended the call just as his deputy hurried in. Cody shook snow from his overcoat and blew on his hands to warm them. "Did you find something?" Murphy asked.

"Not yet." Cody pulled down the map of the area. Gia joined them, and Murphy made the introductions.

"Thanks for helping," Gia said.

"I really like your sister," Cody said sheepishly. "I want to find her. Everyone in town does."

Murphy suspected that his deputy had a crush on Carly. The worry in his voice indicated he might be right.

Cody pointed to the map. "I've divided the area into quadrants, and then marked those into separate sections as well. I'm meeting volunteers at Bubba's in a few to hand out assignments. For safety sake, we're working in teams. Everyone will have radios and are required to check in on the half hour."

"Good work," Murphy said. "Be sure to emphasize that if they find this guy not to approach him, but instead, to just call in the location. You and I will handle apprehension."

"Copy that." Cody replied. "I figure we'd best start the searches right away. By late afternoon we may have to call a temporary halt because of the weather."

Gia's mouth twitched as if she wanted to argue but refrained. They all knew Holly was a dangerous storm.

"Do you have provisions?" Murphy asked.

His deputy nodded. "Bubba and Arlene are making sandwiches and thermoses of hot coffee for us. They said they'll be open as long as we have crews that need to be fed."

Cody handed Murphy a printout of the grid system, along with names of the team members.

"This way you'll know everyone's location in case we need to touch base," he said.

Gia thanked him again, and Murphy walked his deputy to the door. "Good luck out there. And be careful, man."

Cody tugged his coat around his neck, stepped outside, then climbed in his Jeep to head to Bubba's.

"I'd forgotten what a close-knit community Tinley is," Gia murmured, touched by Cody's concern and quick actions.

"It's one reason I stay," Murphy said. "I like the sense of community." And he couldn't bear to leave his mother.

"My partner is investigating Dr. Whitman," Gia continued, "and I asked him to have our analysts review footage or persons of interest they've already questioned then look at their occupations." She folded her arms. "The travel aspect was a good call, Murph."

Murphy shrugged. "I hope it pans out." He snagged his keys from his desk. "I talked to our local real estate agency. She's gathering a list of everyone renting cottages or rooms at the inn this week."

"Good. I'll send that list to my partner as well."

Murphy pulled on his gloves. "Whitman looked at a couple of properties. I think we should check them out."

Gia ran a hand over her hair. Her ponytail was sagging, strands slipping out, and she tightened the band.

For a fraction of a second, Murphy envisioned threading his fingers through the silky strands. Not the right time though.

Oblivious, Gia was all business. "Let me change my clothes."

Murphy retrieved her suitcase, and she slipped into the bathroom. When she came out, she was dressed in jeans, a warm winter sweater, gloves, hat and snow boots. She yanked on her coat. "Let's go."

He nodded and opened the door. They didn't have time to waste. Holly was gaining momentum.

Carly's life depended on them acting quickly.

CHAPTER THIRTEEN

9:00 A.M., December 19, Tinley

GIA RUBBED her arms with her hands as Murphy drove through town. The wind battered his vehicle, and he cranked up the defroster, although even with it running full force, visibility impeded the trek.

The only snowplow and salting truck in town had cleared the main road, but hadn't covered the side roads yet, so they were icing over, snow accumulating and piling into drifts. Tinley just wasn't as prepared as the bigger cities in Nebraska.

Even those who were ready would be buried in snow by tonight. The shady areas and lack of sun would prevent the snow from melting during the day, and the roads would turn to black ice.

As Murphy passed Bubba's, Gia's heart squeezed at the sight of the people who'd left the warmth of their homes and families to search for Carly. He turned onto First Street and drove past the local mercantile, which had a few cars in the lot as people rushed to stock up on last minute supplies. Next door was an outfitters store, then the building at the end was vacant.

Murphy parked in front of it, and she scanned the street and property. It was a plain brick building that had once housed a clothing factory that had filed bankruptcy and closed five years ago.

Gia checked that her weapon, then reached for the door handle. "Do you have a key?"

"No, but the realtor texted me the code for the lock box."

Together they climbed out, alert for any indication someone was inside. Gia's snow boots sank into the thick sludge as she approached the building. Rectangular windows flanked the door, and Murphy checked the left one while she peeked inside the right.

She struggled to see through the dark interior but could only make out the front space which appeared empty.

Murphy punched in the code Lea had texted him, retrieved the key to the building then unlocked the door. She pulled her gun and braced it at the ready. Murphy did the same. He motioned to let him go first, and she stepped to the side to cover him.

He entered slowly then stepped to the left and she followed, pausing in the entryway to listen for sounds that Carly, or the CK, was inside. No voices, just a hollow echo of the wind howling through the old eaves. Dust motes swirled like tiny bugs in front of her eyes as she gestured at the hallway nearest her. Murphy went the opposite direction, his wet boots squeaking.

She came to a large room that was empty, then crept toward two smaller rooms. A door led to what was probably once a storage closet.

She held her breath as she opened it and looked inside. Carly wasn't there. Neither was the killer.

Footsteps pounded, then Murphy's voice. "Clear."

"Clear."

Emotions pummeled her as they met in the front entryway again. She'd been terrified she'd find Carly dead and posed like the others.

Still, where was her sister?

9:20 A.M., DECEMBER 19, TINLEY

Tension vibrated in the car, intensified by the pounding wind and cold. Murphy clenched the steering wheel in a white-knuckled grip and flipped on the radio for an update on the weather.

"The temperature is rapidly dropping, and by nightfall, we expect to reach a low of minus ten with a wind chill of thirty below. People, please stay home. Roads are quickly becoming dangerous. Even a short time out in this kind of cold can cause hypothermia and be deadly."

A pause, then the announcer. "Now, for more news. FBI and local police are searching for a missing woman named Carly Franklin from Tinley. Police believe she was kidnapped by the notorious Christmas Killer and are asking for anyone with information regarding the young woman's disappearance or the whereabouts of the Christmas Killer to call authorities."

Gia sighed and looked out the window, and he turned off the radio. Frost clung to the glass, creating spider-like webs on the pane. The SUV chugged over the snow packed ground, the wind trying to yank it off the road.

Murphy turned onto Old Mill Road, slowing as he fought the keep the vehicle steady. Though the road was paved, it led out to farmland and was a rocky ride on a good day. Today it was treacherous.

Gia gripped the door edge as he swerved to avoid some fallen limbs. The houses in the area were spaced farther apart, some a half-acre while others sat on an acre or more. Most were older ranches and farmhouses that had been built in the nineteen fifties and sixties, although a few buyers had torn down the old homesteads and built new homes on the sprawling flat land.

Just before they reached the Franklin house, Murphy veered into the drive of the house Whitman had looked at, a rustic farmhouse in dark gray.

Pain wrenched Gia's face as he parked. "Dear heavens, Murph, he looked at the house beside ours." She turned to him, fear darkening her eyes. "He chose his other victims at random, but Carly...he chose because of me. And if Whitman is the perp, he came here and stalked her."

9:30 A.M., DECEMBER 19, TINLEY

Gia hadn't considered the consequences of her job on her family, that she was putting her loved ones—her *only* family member—in danger.

If she had, would she have become an agent?

All Carly wanted was for you to come home and decorate the tree with her. And now you might not ever get to see her again. Or tell her how much you love her.

"Gia?" Murphy's deep voice cut into her troubled thoughts. "If you want to wait here, I'll check out the house."

Gia swiped at a tear she hadn't realized had slipped down her cheek. "No. I'm going with you." She settled her hand over her gun as she climbed from the vehicle. The vicious wind slapped her in the face; snow froze on her cheeks.

Bracing herself for an ambush, she and Murphy slogged through the snow to the front porch of the house. The stairs were rickety and slick, covered in snow and ice. She gripped the handrail to keep from falling.

Murphy motioned that he would go around back, and she gestured in understanding. When she reached the porch landing, she squinted through the front window. The house was dark, but she spotted a large den and kitchen.

Both appeared empty.

Gia knew she had to be careful though. She pulled her gun and jiggled the doorknob. Locked. Gritting her teeth, she removed a hairpin from beneath her ponytail and picked the lock. Treading quietly, she pushed the door open and stepped inside.

Without heat on, the house seemed almost as cold as the outdoors, and the floor creaked. Then an acrid odor hit her.

The smell of death.

She froze, immobilized by fear and what might lay in wait for her inside. The sound of the back door bursting open startled her. She pivoted and aimed her gun.

Murphy stood in the hallway, his gun drawn, his expression stony as he surveyed the rooms on both sides of the hall. She sagged in relief and lowered her gun.

Then she quickly searched the kitchen and laundry room. The house had been deserted for some time. The few pieces of furniture that had been left were dusty and moldy.

Murphy hooked a finger toward a hallway door that led to a downstairs.

She held her breath as she hurried down the hall and followed him into the dark basement.

CHAPTER FOURTEEN

9:35 A.M., December 19, Tinley

THE EARLY BIRD *catches the worm.* That's what his mama used to say.

And he'd caught it this morning, long before anyone was out and about in Tinley.

He knocked snow off his coat and shoes as he slipped inside his safe haven.

Yesterday, he'd heard the whiners complaining about how the blizzard was ruining the Christmas Festival. The arts and craft show, the carolers, carriage rides with Santa, the Christmas pageant, the holiday shopping and the Christmas cookie bake-off—all had been postponed. Who knew if they would even reschedule?

If the town became buried in snow, it could take a week to dig itself out. People would be trapped. Stranded on the road.

Which would make it more difficult for him to leave town, too.

Except he would leave.

And he had the perfect place to hide until then.

A place that roused both good and bad memories.

As he closed the door to the shed, the scent of sugar, buttercream frosting and brownies from Sari's kitchen clung to him. He paused to trace a finger over the photograph he'd snapped of her after he'd finished posing her. Her soft blonde hair had felt decadent across his fingers.

He smiled at the image. Sweet Sari made treats for the town. Sweet Sari would do so no more.

Only he'd left her sitting at her worktable with sugar cookie dough rolled out onto the cutting board, her hand pressing the Christmas star cookie cutter into the dough as if her joyous task had been interrupted. Before he left, he'd drizzled rainbow sprinkles across the dough to add to the holiday mood and left her radio playing Christmas carols.

The shiny red ribbon he'd used to tie the ten lords-a-leaping ornament to her wrist looked festive against her pale skin.

It was his best photograph yet. True art.

He sighed and walked over to where Carly lay. Gently he brushed her hair from her cheek and watched her eyelashes flutter in sleep.

"Don't worry, I'll make you beautiful, too," he murmured. Then he set the picture of Sari on the table beside the bed where Carly slept, so she could see it when she woke up.

CHAPTER FIFTEEN

9:45 A.M., December 19, Tinley

WIND SLASHED the outside of the old house, the loose shutters flapping against rotting wood.

Murphy gestured to Gia for her to let him go down the steps first. Granted, she was FBI, but this case was personal to her, and his protective instincts reared their head.

She pinched her lips together into a firm scowl. He wasn't sure if she was angry with him for taking charge or with herself for struggling to school her emotions.

Even in high school, Gia had been tough. The athlete. Not the girl to sit on the bench or bat her eyelashes and play helpless like some of the girls who used their feminine charm to make men fall at their feet. Then again, sometimes he'd seen glimpses that Gia might have a tender side beneath the hard surface.

Her toughness could be an act though. Being the older of the sisters, she'd probably felt compelled to take care of her younger sibling. Worry and uncertainty must be killing her now.

The ancient steps creaked as he inched down them, the acrid odor growing stronger. Behind him, Gia's sharp breath indicated she recognized the fetid smell of death below.

As he shone his flashlight across the dank space, dust motes floated in the hazy dim light.

"Carly?" Gia whispered. "Are you down here, honey?"

The sound of her pained voice echoed in the desolate quiet. He swept the flashlight to the right. Tattered cardboard boxes and newspapers were stacked against the wall. An antique dresser sat on three legs, the mirror cracked and spotted with grime.

He crept down another step, then another, until they reached the landing.

He waved the flashlight across the room. More boxes overflowing with junk, then an old refrigerator and stove on the opposite wall.

He couldn't see anyone visible. No closets or separate rooms, indicating the basement had never been finished.

"The refrigerator," Gia croaked.

He gave a quick nod, then started across the space. The cement floor was coated in years of dust and dirt, and something sticky. He glanced down to see what it was. Blood.

Gia moved ahead of him, shining her own light in the direction of the refrigerator.

So far, the Christmas Killer had left his victims posed as if putting on a show, not hidden inside somewhere. He'd strangled them instead of using a knife or gun, which made the crime scene less messy.

Here, a big puddle of blood stained the floor.

Although if the killer's goal was to torture Gia, he could have altered his MO.

Ashen-faced, she slowly pulled on the refrigerator door

handle. A second later, she jumped back, a cry escaping her as a bloody carcass fell from the interior.

9:50 A.M., DECEMBER 19, TINLEY

Gia made a choking sound and jumped back. For a second, she stood in shock then relief slowly seeped through her.

The carcass was a dead deer. Not her sister. Not Carly.

Thank God.

"What the hell?" Murphy muttered. "Someone killed the deer, then put it in here without even dressing it."

"I can't believe the real estate agent showed the house like this," Gia said, recovering slightly. "I smelled this the minute we walked through the door."

"I did, too. Maybe someone put the animal in here after she showed it."

Gia covered her mouth with her hand and nose to help ward off the stench. "Let's get out of here."

She hurried toward the stairs, and Murphy followed. When they made it to the outside of the house, she welcomed the blast of cold and inhaled several deep breaths to stem the nausea.

Murphy laid his hand on her shoulder and squeezed gently, and she leaned into him, grateful to have him nearby. Murphy had always been a rock. Solid and stable and ...so sexy that she'd been afraid if she'd leaned on him years ago and stayed in town, she never would have left.

She squeezed his hand, then squared her shoulders to let him know she was okay.

Understanding passed between them. There was something there, a chemistry they couldn't deny. But now wasn't the time. Finding Carly was all that mattered.

Murphy stepped away, then made a call. "Tamika, this is Sheriff Malone," he said. "Please call me ASAP."

Gia gripped the handrail and trudged down the steps. She had to get away from that house. From the sight of that bloody dead animal.

But she couldn't escape the fear clawing at her.

She and Murphy battled the blustery wind as they climbed in his SUV. "You didn't talk to Tamika?"

"She didn't answer. Which is odd. Her assistant said she was working from home today."

Gia's heart stuttered. "Maybe you should check her house."

Murphy's gaze cut to her. "You're worried about her?"

"If she showed the vet this house, and he's our killer, then she can recognize him. That would be motive for him to add her to his list."

Concern shadowed his dark eyes. "True. Although if Dr. Whitman is the CK, I met him and so did several locals. We could all identify him."

"Tamika might have picked up on something when she showed him the properties."

"That's possible. Let's head over there."

Gia touched his arm. "Murph, drop me at my house, I mean Carly's. I'll see if she's there or if I can find anything indicating he's been inside. You check out Tamika's."

Murphy wheezed a breath. "I don't want to leave you alone, Gia. This maniac is after you."

"I appreciate your concern, but he has Carly. And we can't waste time. We can cover more ground by dividing up."

Murphy looked as if he wanted to argue, but he was smart and knew she was right. "Okay," he said, his voice heavy with apprehension. "But if he shows up, call me for back up."

She patted her weapon, which she'd stowed inside her jacket. "I have back up right here."

His jaw tightened, and he started the engine, maneuvered the drive, then turned onto the country road. Snow whirled in a blinding haze, frost and ice spreading across the front window in a pattern that resembled broken glass.

Her parents' homestead sat on the acre lot next door to the house they'd just searched. Murphy turned into the drive, and Gia blinked back tears.

So many memories here. So many happy times with her sister and mother.

So much sadness when her mother died.

She could not bury her sister, too.

10:00 A.M., DECEMBER 19, TINLEY

Murphy parked in front of the Franklin house, his shoulders knotted with tension. Snow stood over two feet deep in front of the sprawling farmhouse, coating the steps to the wrap around porch, and icicles clung to the awning. The trees in front of the property swayed in the storm, the branches bowed and heavy with snow and ice.

He'd always thought this property was beautiful, but today it looked almost eerie, haunted.

"I'll go in and do a quick search with you," Murphy said.

Gia offered him a brave smile. "No, I ...need to go in alone. Check on Tamika and let me know what you find."

Murphy had the insane urge to drag her into his arms and hold her. To assure her everything would be all right.

But he couldn't do that, not when he didn't know if her sister was alive or dead.

"Go," Gia said, her tone commanding this time. "If Tamika is in trouble, she needs you."

Murphy nodded, his chest tight with anxiety as she

jumped from his SUV and plowed through the snow up to her porch. He told himself she was a trained agent, and she was armed.

Gia was right. If the killer had targeted Tamika, it might not be too late to save her. But if she was unharmed, she might have insight as to whether Whitman was the CK.

Gripping the steering wheel, he shifted into reverse, turned around and headed toward Tamika's house. She lived about a block from town in a bungalow near her real estate office.

His phone buzzed. Cody.

He quickly connected. "Yeah? Did you find Carly?"

Static popped and crackled, the blizzard already messing with phone reception and the only nearby cell tower.

"Afraid not." Cody's voice warbled in and out with the wind battering the connection. "One of our teams found a family trapped in their car. They skidded into a ditch and have been there for a few hours. A rescue team is digging them out now."

Perspiration beaded on Murphy's neck. "Send a team out to the cottages and have them look by the creek. Is Judah Willingham with you?" Judah had been a deputy in the county for twenty years before he retired.

"He was first to volunteer."

Murphy chuckled. "Deputize him and have him go door to door with you. Also, canvass the people staying at the cottages. Maybe someone saw something. Or—"

"Or see if the killer is holding Carly there," Cody finished. "On it."

Murphy thanked him, his snow tires churning as he swung into the drive for Tamika's bungalow. He scanned the small yard and property but didn't see anything suspicious. The garage door was shut. Was Tamika's car inside?

He parked and climbed out, weapon clenched by his side

as he hiked through the snow and climbed the steps to her porch. A welcome sign dangled precariously in the violent wind. A loose shudder flapped. The watering can on the porch had blown over and was rolling across the wood planks.

A light glowed from inside, indicating someone might be home. He raised his gloved hand and knocked on the door.

"Tamika," he shouted, "if you're in there, please open up." He stepped to the side and peeked through a front window. A shadow moved. His hand inched to his gun as he waited.

A minute later, the door screeched open, and Tamika appeared, burrowed in a big terry cloth robe. "Sheriff? What are you doing here?"

Murphy shifted and tried to look behind her. There was someone there. Was he holding Tamika against her will? "Just checking to see if you're all right."

Her thick black brows bunched as she frowned. "I'm good. Why shouldn't I be?"

"You heard the news about Carly?"

"Yes, that's awful," she said, her voice softening.

"Tamika, sweet babe, are you coming back to bed?" a man called.

Murphy recognized the voice. Devon Boles who owned the hardware store.

"Yes, I'll be right there." A blush stole across her ebony cheeks.

Murphy smiled. He hadn't realized Devon and Tamika were seeing each other. "Looks like I interrupted something."

Tamika toyed with her waist-length braid. "Figured we all had a day off cause of the storm. Although Devon left his assistant at the hardware store for people needing emergency supplies." She curled a hand around the door. "Why are you really here, Sheriff?"

"Like I said, it's about that killer we think is in town."

Fear flashed across the young woman's face. "You think he's after me?"

"No, but you should stay with Devon until we catch him. At the moment, I'm considering a lot of possibilities. He took Carly, we know that. I also saw her with that vet who came to town a couple of times. You showed him some property?"

"Yes, an abandoned warehouse and the house neighboring the Franklin's. I don't think he was ready to commit though."

"What was your impression of him?" Murphy asked.

Tamika scrunched her nose in thought. "He was nice enough, I guess. Seemed like he was on the fence about moving."

"Did he ever say or do anything suspicious when you were with him?"

Tamika cinched the belt around her robe. "Not really. I just think he was torn about relocating and not ready to commit."

Because he hadn't really planned to move there?

"You said you showed him the house beside the Franklin's?"

Tamika's eyes widened as she connected the dots. "Oh, heavens, you think he was staking out Carly's house, that he used me to get close?"

Murphy shrugged. "It's possible." His phone buzzed, and he glanced at it wondering if it was Gia. No. Arlene.

"Tamika, think about it, if Whitman said or did anything that made you think he might be dangerous. Or if he might have been probing you for information about Carly and her sister."

"I will. Good luck finding her, Sheriff." Fear clouded her expression as she closed the door.

Murphy connected the call. "Hello."

"Sheriff, it's Arlene over at Bubba's."

"Yeah."

"I may be overreacting, but Sari was supposed to deliver some pies to the café today and she hasn't shown with them."

"She probably decided to stay home because of the weather," Murphy said.

"Could be. But last night, she said she'd already baked the pies and she insisted she'd drop them off early, so I'd have them for the search crews. She really wanted to help."

That sounded like Sari.

"Anyway, Bubba walked down to the sweet shop and she's not there."

A frisson of alarm ripped through Murphy. Sari was young. Pretty. Lived alone.

What if the CK had chosen her as his tenth victim?

CHAPTER SIXTEEN

10:10 A.M., December 19, Tinley

GIA SLID her hand into her pocket and placed it over her service weapon as she reached the front door of her family home.

Beverly Franklin hated guns of all kinds and would probably be appalled she was bringing one into the house today. She'd emphasized family dinners, togetherness, and helping your neighbors. There was always room for one more at the table.

Then she'd died and left an empty hole in Gia's heart. She'd turned her grief and anger into motivation that had made her throw herself into work and hunting down bad guys.

She would want you to find Carly.

That thought lessened the guilt for the gun.

A wind blast pummeled the windows, and ice cracked and snapped from the trees, flying downward. She jiggled the door, but it was locked. She'd left her key for the house back in Florida.

Remembering that her mother always left an extra one beneath the flowerpot, she checked it in case Carly followed suit. A smile tugged at her mouth as her fingers raked over the metal.

People in Tinley never locked their doors and trusted their neighbors.

That would change after this was over. A predator on the prowl in your hometown tended to destroy trust and incite suspicion. Not a good thing.

But necessary.

She hated that she'd brought that dark cloud to Tinley.

Gia unlocked the door, then eased it open and peered inside in case the killer was waiting in ambush. That had happened to her once early on in the job. She'd ended up with six stitches in the back of her head and the perp had escaped.

The ancient furnace rumbled, working hard to heat the interior of the farmhouse and failing. When she found Carly and brought her home, she'd install a new HVAC system.

Emotions clogged her throat as she spotted the balsam fir perched in front of the window facing the front porch. Carly had strung garland along the limbs, yet the box of family ornaments, ones she and her sister had handcrafted with their mother, sat on the floor by the wall waiting to be added.

Carly wanted the two of you to decorate together.

But you were too busy. Always too busy.

Fear and regret stole the air from her lungs. But she didn't have time to break down. She wasn't here for a trip down memory lane. That could come later.

She needed to look around, hunt for any hint the killer had been inside.

She jerked her gaze away from the tree and moved into the den, which opened to the kitchen and dining area.

Christmas decorations adorned the wall and house, each one a reminder that Carly was continuing the family traditions while she'd abandoned them.

Her mother's collection of Santas lined the mantle. Another table held Christmas cottages and snow globes. The family pictures of her and Carly when they were little standing by the Christmas tree in their holiday pajamas were arranged on the bookcase. The yearly photos of the two of them in the sleigh at the tree farm occupied an entire shelf. Silver bells and mistletoe dangled from the doors. Red, green and gold candles dotted the bathroom and kitchen counter. The scent of apple pie wafted from the candle on the breakfast bar.

A scrapbook on the kitchen counter drew her eye and she walked over to examine it. Curious, she opened it.

Inside, the pages were filled with articles covering each case she'd worked. Other pages held photographs from various press conferences and news events where she'd briefed the public.

Was her sister keeping up with her career by collecting these?

She turned the last few pages and discovered articles about the Christmas Killer.

Then on the last page—a copy of the lyrics to "The Twelve Days of Christmas."

10:30 A.M., DECEMBER 19, TINLEY

Murphy decided to stop by Sari's Sweet Shop before checking her house. Sari usually arrived at the shop by dawn to start baking for the day. He checked the rear parking lot for her car as he drove up, but the parking lot was empty.

So were the streets, a good sign people were heeding the warning about the hazardous weather conditions. The Christmas garland and strands of lights the town had put up were battering the light posts and storefronts as the wind gusts intensified.

Today would have been the parade with floats, music and food trucks in the town square. Instead, the downtown area looked like a ghost town buried in white.

The only businesses that had opened were the hardware store and Bubba's. The financial loss would hurt.

But right now, he was more concerned about a killer on the loose.

He parked in front of the store, buttoned his coat and yanked on his winter hat then hiked through the snow to the front entrance. The glass door was coated in an icy fog, so he wiped at it with his glove then peered inside.

The interior was dark. No movement inside.

The memory of finding blood in Carly's shop taunted him, and he circled to the back door and checked the door. Locked.

He picked the lock, then pushed open the door. He paused to listen as he entered. Silence greeted him along with the smell of cinnamon, gingerbread and chocolate.

He kicked snow off his boots and walked through the hallway, peering into the storage room where Sari kept baking supplies. Next he checked the walk-in refrigerator/freezer. Relieved to find cooking ingredients, frozen cookies and cakes instead of Sari, he inched through the hall to the front of the store. The glass cabinet that held pastries was stocked with a few treats, but the tables were clean, chairs stacked, counter empty, indicating Sari hadn't come in at all today.

Perhaps she'd baked those pies at home and was snowed in.

Unless...the CK had gone to her house.

He gripped his keys and hurried out the back door and locked it. His cell phone buzzed as he climbed back in his SUV. Gia.

"Hey," he said as he connected and started the engine.

"He was here, Murph."

Murphy went bone still. "At Carly's?"

"Yes."

"Is he there now?"

"No and no sign of my sister. But he left a scrapbook, articles of all the cases I've worked and ones covering the Christmas Killer case." Agitation shattered her normally calm voice. "He also left a copy of the lyrics to 'The Twelve Days of Christmas' in the album."

"I'm on the way." Murphy spun in the direction of the Franklin house. "Listen, Gia, Arlene called. She was expecting Sari to show up with pastries, but she hasn't seen or heard from her. I checked the Sweet Shop and she's not there. I was going to drive out to her house now. I'll swing by and pick you up."

GIA HUNG up and said a silent prayer that Sari was okay. Then she hurried to search the rest of the house as she waited on Murphy.

Careful to use gloves, she checked the bookshelf, but the photographs of she and her family seemed to be in place.

Carly hadn't changed the den or kitchen, but she'd painted the master bedroom a soft blue and thrown a blue and white quilt in a snowflake pattern over the bed. A darker shade of blue covered the master bath walls, with pictures of lilies over the claw foot tub. The room looked soft and feminine and sweet, just like her sister.

A sharp pang of fear sliced through her, but she forced herself to breathe through the pain.

Pulse pounding, she checked the drawers and closet, but nothing seemed out of place. Not that she expected anything to be missing.

The CK's MO didn't include theft or vandalism. He didn't rape or torture his victims. He simply strangled them and posed them with the Christmas ornaments.

She examined the bathroom then the second bedroom that used to belong to her and Carly. A queen white iron bed draped in a red and green poinsettia quilt had replaced the twin beds.

She'd painted the room a muted shade of sage green.

Gia's favorite color.

Tears blinded her. Carly had redone the room for her. And she'd been too selfish to come home and see it.

She swiped at her eyes.

Satisfied the bedrooms were intact, she walked down the hall to the living room again. The empty tree and the box of ornaments mocked her from the floor.

Each year her mother had made ornaments with them, some out of paper or plastic, some wooden that they'd bought at the craft store and painted. They'd used glitter and sequins and shiny stones to add sparkle.

She and Carly had loved the annual tree decorating parties. Christmas music filled the room while they strung popcorn. When the tree was lit up and glowing, they nibbled on homemade cookies and sipped hot chocolate.

Emotions threatened to overcome her again. She shook them off. She had to focus.

Get inside the killer's head, figure out what made him tick.

The Twelve Days song echoed in her head.

Her mother had once told her the story of the song, that

each day the mother gave her child a gift, and each day the gifts grew more lavish.

That song, the story, had to mean something to the killer.

But what exactly?

A knock sounded on the door, and she hurried to let Murphy inside. "I called a crime team from the county to come and process the house."

"We need to send this to the lab as soon as possible." She gestured to the scrapbook which she'd already placed in a plastic bag, then told Murphy to text the team with instructions on where to find the house key.

As soon as he sent the text, she locked up and they hurried outside, then down the steps and into his SUV. Silence stretched between them as Murphy drove, the drone of the windshield wipers, defroster and battering wind adding to the tension.

"How well do you know Sari?" Gia finally asked.

Murphy shrugged. "Just through the shop. She's in her mid-twenties, loves baking, and opened the shop in town to be close by her grandmother. The old lady died last year."

Gia bit her bottom lip. "Was Sari dating anyone?"

"I don't know much about her personal life. Arlene or one of the teenagers she hired to work for her might know."

Gia drummed her fingers on her thigh. Her head was throbbing from lack of sleep, her muscles aching. If they found Sari alive and safe, they wouldn't need to ask about her private life.

Murphy turned down Second Street, passed a couple of small bungalows, then stopped at the third driveway. A white Craftsman with bright blue shutters and a red door.

Gia scanned the property. A white minivan with the logo of Sari's Sweets emblazoned on the side sat in the drive.

"Does she own another vehicle?" Gia asked.

Murphy shook his head, parked and cut the engine. Gia

slid her hand over her weapon again, secured her hat and scarf, then climbed out. In spite of her thick winter coat, the wind chill ripped through her, biting all the way to her bones. If there was a sidewalk, it was buried in the snow.

She reminded herself to breathe as they slogged to the front door. The Christmas wreath bore tiny red birds, but the wind had unraveled the gold bow and it dangled downward against the door-frame.

Murphy raised his fist and pounded on the door. "Sari, it's the sheriff. Open up."

No answer. No voices or footsteps. Just the shrill wind slicing through the air. Murphy knocked again, and Gia pulled her weapon and started around the side of the house. She checked the windows as she circled to the back, but the curtains were drawn, obscuring her view.

A back patio held a small round patio table covered in snow, fallen twigs and debris.

She climbed the one step to the stoop and peered through the window.

Sari sat at the kitchen worktable with her back to the door. She was so still that a chill of foreboding rippled up Gia's spine.

She twisted at the doorknob and the door swung open, the force of the wind practically pushing Gia inside. She paused at the threshold then fought to close the door.

The scent of death mingled with the sugary scent of cookie dough.

Gripping her weapon, she crept up by Sari's side, then walked around to face her. She choked back a cry.

They were too late.

TINLEY 7 NEWS

Meteorologist Bailey Huggins ducked as a tree branch snapped off and sailed downward, nearly catching her in the head. She'd known reporting could be dangerous but hadn't realized the weather would be the threat.

"Just look around here, folks," she said into the camera as she gestured at the foot-high snowdrifts along the streets of Tinley. "Holly, the worst blizzard in our history, is clobbering us right now with wind gusts up to 65 miles per hour and heavy snowfall reaching twelve inches and climbing. Unfortunately, there's no relief in sight. She shivered against the wind, then continued, "Already businesses, government offices, stores and shops have shut down. Hotels and inns are overflowing with stranded tourists, the airport is filled with holiday travelers forced to hole up inside, and whiteout conditions have made roads impassable. No-travel advisories have been issued for the state, and all flights in and out of Omaha have been cancelled."

She paused, hunching deeper inside her down coat as the wind blasted her and whipped her wool scar around her face. "Meteorologists have dubbed this storm as a bomb cyclone because of its rapidly intensifying funnel shape. Downed power lines, roofs collapsing due to heavy snowfall, power outages, traffic accidents and freezing temperatures have already accounted for ten deaths in the state.

"Typically snow invites children to sled or play in the drifts, but conditions are extremely dangerous now, so please keep them inside. The temperature has already dropped below zero and is rapidly declining, with a wind chill factor expected to reach a record thirty below." She exhaled, her breath puffing out in a white cloud.

"Damages to property, cattle and crops are expected to be significant, reaching well over a million dollars. Possible tornados and flooding as the snow begins to melt pose another danger."

She forced a smile and felt like it was freezing on her face. "Yes, it sounds like a dismal Christmas this year, but please stay hunkered inside and keep warm. The worst is expected to make a direct hit on Tinley within the next few hours, so stay safe.

"This is Bailey Huggins, signing off from Channel 7 Tinley News, wishing you a safe and happy holiday."

Grateful to end the segment, she hurried to the news van, anxious to feel the heat and her toes again. She just hoped people heeded the warnings and she didn't have to report any more weather-related casualties.

CHAPTER SEVENTEEN

10:45 A.M., December 19, Tinley

FOOTSTEPS POUNDED on the wood floor, and wind blasted through the room coming from the front door.

The moment Murphy saw Sari's body, he halted. "Dear God." Although they both knew Sari was dead, he pressed two fingers gently to her wrist to check for a pulse.

Murphy shook his head, emotions clouding his eyes. "She was a nice girl, dammit. She never did anything to hurt anyone."

"They were all so young," Gia said, her chest so tight she could barely breathe. "They had so much to look forward to." Just as her sister did.

"It's all my fault. I brought this killer here to Tinley. He killed Sari and took Carly to hurt me." Exhaustion, grief and guilt collapsed on top of Gia, and her legs buckled.

Murphy's strong hands gripped her arms, and he pulled her up against him. "Steady now. Take a deep breath."

Gia's body trembled. "It's true. Sari's dead now because of me. And Carly...what if he's already—"

"Shh, don't," Murphy murmured. "He's toying with you, getting inside your head." He rubbed slow circles over her back. "Don't let him in there, Gia. You're strong."

Angry tears clogged her throat. "But it's my fault Sari is dead," she cried.

Murphy tilted her chin up. "Listen to me. She is *not* dead because of you. She's dead because a crazed psycho is out there hunting innocent women."

"And he's here in your town because of *me*." There was no denying that, so he didn't bother.

Instead, he pulled her to him once again, and whispered comforting words. Although nothing he could say could alleviate the guilt weighing on her. They stood there for several long seconds, entrenched in anguish and the shock of finding another young woman's life snuffed out.

"Gia, you're going to get through this, and we will find Carly," Murphy rasped. "I know it's difficult, but we have to focus right now."

His calm authority renewed her strength. He was right.

She slowly lifted her head, her vision blurring. Murphy whispered her name, then gently wiped at the tears streaming down her cheek.

"You're right, thank you, Murphy." For a second, their gazes locked. She wanted more. To fall into his arms again, and this time to stay there. To kiss him. To have him make this nightmare go away.

But she simply nodded and pulled herself together.

Murphy released her, then glanced around the room. "I'll search the house." He didn't bother to wait for a response. He strode from the room into the hall and disappeared out of sight.

Guilt and sorrow welled in Gia's chest, and she gulped back a sob.

You have to stop this crazy lunatic. Make him pay for what he's done.

The only way to do that was to work the crime scene.

She took a deep, fortifying breath, then removed her phone and began snapping pictures of the way Sari was posed. The pale lines of her face looked stark against the red scarf, her lifeless body a macabre sight with her hand on that damn cookie cutter.

Footsteps echoed from the hall, then Murphy's voice as he returned. "Clear."

She gave him a quick glance, then captured close-ups of the items on the table, including Sari's fingers. Was it possible she'd fought back and gotten some DNA beneath those nails?

They hadn't found DNA with the other victims, but Sari could have wrestled with him.

"You've seen all of the victims at the crime scenes," Murphy said, cutting into her thoughts. "Is it the same perp?"

"The MO is identical, so I'd say it's him. We never released photos or details about the red scarf and ribbon."

Gia removed her winter gloves then pulled on latex ones. She visually swept the room for clues, willing the killer to have lost a button or left a stray hair.

At first glance, she saw nothing. No blood on the body or anywhere else. Just the red scarf wound around Sari's neck and the Ten Lords-a-Leaping ornament tied to her wrist.

Gia eased the scarf slightly down for a closer inspection of Sari's neck. The strangle marks, red and deep, matched the ones from the other victims. Forensics would have to compare the exact depth and width of the impressions to verify they were made by the same person, but they appeared to be the same. She photographed the wound so she could email the image to her team.

"I'll call the ME and ERT, then secure the scene." He hurried outside to retrieve the crime scene tape and make the call.

Gia began to examine Sari's body more closely. Her pulse jumped when she spotted a short dark hair.

Sari's hair was red.

If this one belonged to the killer, the DNA might lead them straight to him.

10:50 A.M., DECEMBER 19, TINLEY

Murphy phoned the ERT and relayed the situation as he stepped outside.

"We'll be out as soon as possible," the crime tech said. "Right now, we're waiting on the snowplow. The roads are already iced over, and the bridge from Little Creek Road to town is closed."

Murphy thanked him, then called the ME. No answer. He left a message, then grabbed his forensic kit and hurried back into the house. "A team is coming, but I'll see what I can find."

His nerves were on edge as he strode through the rooms of the bungalow. Dammit to hell. He didn't like the fact that one of his own had been murdered.

And Carly was still missing.

Did the number ten ornament tied to Sari's wrist mean Gia's sister was still alive? Was this sicko saving her, waiting to pose her body as his grand finale?

The house had two bedrooms with a Jack and Jill bathroom in between. The first one was set up as an office. Neat and organized with a small desk, file cabinet, bulletin board with fliers Sari had created to advertise the store and specialty items, along with a wall calendar for planning special events for her catering business.

Everything appeared to be in place, so he moved to the bedroom. A green and blue comforter covered a queen bed, and a tall dresser stood in the corner by a full-length mirror. Jewelry box was closed. When he lifted the lid, it was neat and organized as well. No robbery intent to the crime.

Which also fit with the CK.

Even though nothing looked as if it had been touched, he still had to play this by the book. Make sure the crime techs went over every inch of the house. At some point, this guy had to get tired or sloppy and make a mistake.

He walked back into the bathroom and quickly surveyed the sink and counter. Hair products, toiletries, make up. Nothing indicating a male had been here or that Sari had a boyfriend.

Satisfied that the house was clear, he strode back to the kitchen. Gia was examining the table and the cookie dough.

His phone trilled. The medical examiner's office.

The fifty-something-year-old doctor sounded slightly winded. "Sheriff, you left a message?"

"That's right. I hate to drag you out in this blizzard, but I'm at Sari Benedict's house."

"This can't be good," he said grimly.

"It's not. She's dead. The Christmas Killer."

A tense second passed, then a pained sigh. "Ahh, God. Poor Sari."

"I know. We need you to come to her house. I've called a crime team, but it'll be a while before they can get here."

Dr. Nix cleared his throat. "I'll be there as soon as I can." Another tense heartbeat passed. "Murphy, did you find Carly?"

His chest squeezed. "Not yet. We're still searching."

"I'm on my way."

They hung up, and Murphy gritted his teeth as he looked back at Sari.

Gia was bent over examining the woman's neck more closely, then her hands.

"ME's on his way."

She gave a little nod, then lifted a baggie. "I found a hair, Murphy. It's short and dark. Not Sari's."

His pulse jumped. "Then it could be the killer's."

Finally, a lead. He just hoped it wasn't too late for Gia's sister.

11:00 A.M., DECEMBER 19, TINLEY

Gia hoped to hell the DNA from the hair gave them a name. But time was of the essence. Getting it to the lab with the bad weather hampering travel would take time.

"I'm going to look around outside," Murphy said. "See if I find any footprints or tire tracks. The killer had to get in and out of here some way."

Gia considered his comment. If there had been footprints or tire tracks, the snow had probably buried them. Still, she appreciated Murphy's diligence. Some small-town sheriffs she'd worked with hated the FBI encroaching on their territory.

Others weren't quite as on-the-ball professionally.

Murphy was professional, intelligent and observant. He had the mind of a good detective. He could have made it in the Bureau if he'd chosen that route. But seeing him here, connecting to people, treating the town as his family, fit him well. She admired him for his convictions, for ...having heart. So may agents and law enforcement officers and detectives became desensitized.

A cold blast of air engulfed her as Murphy stepped outside, and he shoved at the back door to shut it.

She turned back to the room and surveyed it again.

The image of Sari in that red scarf and apron with the ornament tied to her wrist as she pressed the cookie cutter into the dough was imprinted in her brain forever.

One by one the crime scene photos of the other victims flashed through her head.

Something had happened around the holidays to trigger this mad man to murder. The loss of a child? A spouse?

The ornaments were also significant. Had his family decorated lavishly and given nice gifts for the holidays? Or had they shunned Christmas, and the ornaments represented the kind of gift giving he'd dreamed of?

She punched Brantley's number, and leaned over to study the table again. Something about the cookie dough was bothering her.

"Gia?" Her partner's voice echoed back, although static popped, indicating a bad connection.

"We have victim number ten."

A tense second passed, then a sigh. "Carly?"

"No," Gia said, relief pouring through her voice. Guilt followed for her selfishness. But Carly was her sister. "She's still missing. He killed a young woman named Sari Benedict. She owns the local bakery."

"You're certain it's him?"

"Yes. I'm sending you pics when we hang up."

Brantley cursed. "I'm sorry, Gia. I wish I was there to help."

"It's fine. The sheriff is an asset. He also knows the area and his deputy has formed search parties. The blizzard is complicating the situation though." She explained about the forensics she'd found.

"If the weather's so harsh, how is the perp traveling

around?"

"Good question. Murphy's working on that angle. He's outside now searching for footprints or tire marks. But with all the snow..."

She let the sentence trail off. No need to finish it. Brantley understood.

An indentation in the dough caught her eye, and she leaned closer to examine it. "Tell me you found something on that veterinarian."

"As a matter of fact, I did," her partner answered. "Whitman had a practice in Omaha. Married, no children. Last year he and his wife split right after Thanksgiving."

"The timing could be right. He told the sheriff he was visiting family in Arkansas. Have you located him?"

"No. Found the family he was supposed to be visiting, his folks, but they claim they haven't heard from him in a couple of days."

"Did you check the airports and train stations?" Gia queried.

"I did, but with all the stranded passengers, assessing passenger manifests is a nightmare. I'll keep digging though."

Her heart began to pound. "Can you send me a photograph of him?"

"On its way."

She took a close up shot of the cookie cutter and surrounding dough, then gently lifted the cookie cutter and examined it. Beneath the star shape the dough was indented slightly.

With a fingerprint.

Her heart hammered, and she lifted Sari's hand and studied her long thin fingers, then compared them to the indentation. They were not a match.

Excitement shot through her. Maybe he'd finally messed up and they'd catch this madman after all.

CHAPTER EIGHTEEN

11:00 A.M., December 19, Tinley

THIS KILLER WAS METHODICAL. Nefarious. And cold. Murphy had to get inside his head and think that way as well.

He searched the front stoop and back deck of Sari's house, looking for anything that might be helpful. But snow had blown across both, inches deep.

Sari was in full rigor, indicating it had been hours since she'd died. The killer had probably snuck in and strangled her sometime during the middle of the night. If so, why hadn't there been a struggle? Nothing had been overturned in the bedroom or kitchen. Nothing broken. No signs of wet boot prints or even melted snow on the floor.

Which meant the killer had cleaned up after himself. Made certain to wipe the water away. Cover his footprints.

Murphy searched the trashcan in the garage for a cloth the man could have discarded but found nothing but a bag of trash. He opened it and checked inside, but it contained assorted trash accumulated on a normal daily basis. Used paper towels, an empty toilet paper roll, discarded pizza box, and leftover food that had gone bad.

A recycling bin held boxes and plastic containers from the kitchen. An empty egg carton. Plastic jug that had held milk. Empty bottle of dish soap.

He crossed the garage in search of a broom and found a wet spot near Sari's car. Chest tight, he shined his flashlight along the cement floor and spotted scuffmarks beside the passenger side of the car.

Marks that could belong to Sari. Or the killer.

The killer probably wouldn't have left them if they were his, but maybe he'd been in a hurry. Murphy stooped and photographed them anyway. Careful not to touch anything, he pointed his light on the door handle. Maybe a fingerprint there, although this man had most likely used gloves.

Murphy used gloved hands himself to open the door, then he aimed his flashlight inside the car.

The scent of apple and cinnamon assaulted him, along with cranberries, pumpkin and mincemeat. The pies on the front seat, the ones Sari was supposed to deliver to Bubba's.

He mentally ran a scenario through his head of what had happened. Sari planned to deliver the goodies to Bubba's for the search teams. Expecting the weather to worsen as the day progressed, she'd packed up the pies to deliver early morning.

She'd carried them out to the garage and put them in the car.

The killer had been lying in wait.

11:10 A.M., DECEMBER 19, TINLEY

Gia texted the pictures of the crime scene and the print in the dough to Brantley as soon as they disconnected.

As promised, he sent her a photo of the veterinarian along with his personal information. Parker Whitman was handsome in a GQ sort of way and looked as if he worked out regularly. Did he hone his muscles so he could overtake a woman?

She made a sound of disgust and continued analyzing him. Neatly clipped brown hair, well groomed, a killer smile that probably had women dumping their problems on them in his vet office—or offering to jump into his bed.

Had Carly been charmed by him?

She skimmed the background information. Whitman grew up in a middle-class neighborhood in Little Rock. Although details on him were minimal. Nothing so far about the parents or his upbringing which could play into his motivation. Married a woman two years ago, but it had gone downhill and she'd filed for divorce last November.

A month before Christmas.

That might prove important. But he didn't travel around in his job as Murphy suggested, and there was nothing linking him to the three states in which the CK had chosen to kill.

She needed more information, something specific that pointed to him as the killer.

The sound of a car engine outside jerked her attention toward the front door. Five minutes later, Murphy appeared with the medical examiner.

"Special Agent Franklin, this is Dr. Nix."

He offered his hand, but she held up her gloved hands indicating she'd been working. "Nice to meet you. Hate to drag you out in this mess."

His steely gray eyes matched the silver at his temples. Only those eyes settled on Sari with emotions that suggested he'd met the young woman before and was upset by her death.

"I'm sorry for bringing this killer to Tinley," Gia said, guilt nagging at her.

"Not your fault," the man reassured her. "But it's awful about Sari. She was a great girl." He heaved a breath. "We're all rooting for you and Murphy to find your sister."

Gia murmured thanks. Back to business, she explained about finding the partial print in the cookie dough and relayed the information her partner had passed along.

Murphy relayed his findings in the garage. "It looks as if the snowplow came early this morning and spread salt on the main road, so it may have obliterated any car tire tracks that the snow accumulation didn't cover up."

Dr. Nix tugged on latex gloves, adjusted his glasses and the mic on the collar of his lab coat, then began his initial exam. Gia watched, a feeling of helplessness threatening to overwhelm her as the storm intensified outside.

Ten women had died, and she didn't have a clue as to the killer's identity. What kind of federal agent was she?

Dr. Nix ran a light over Sari's exposed skin searching for signs of violence. Bruises where the psycho had grabbed her discolored her arms. Her hands looked unharmed, but the ME lifted her left one and examined her nails. "I'll scrape for DNA in case she scratched him." He checked Sari's eyes, and Gia recognized signs of petechial hemorrhaging similar to the other victims. Gently, the ME eased away the scarf to examine Sari's neck.

"I'll need to perform the autopsy to confirm, but bruises on her neck and petechial hemorrhaging indicate asphyxiation due to strangulation."

"Same as the other victims. They were injected with a paralytic agent, Pancuronium bromide," Gia said.

"I'll run a full tox screen and check for it." The ME lifted the young woman's hair from the back of Sari's neck and made a low sound in his throat. "Looks like an injection site here."

"The killer came up behind her and jabbed her in the back of the neck before she had a chance to defend herself," Murphy said in a voice laced with disdain.

Gia and Dr. Nix both murmured their agreement. "She never had a chance," Gia said. "The drug rendered her helpless to fight back."

Outside, an engine sounded, and Murphy went to check it out. A minute later, he returned with two techs from the crime lab. "We got here as soon as we could. It's rough out there," Lt. Mason said.

"Oh, my word." The female's face turned ashen. "That serial killer really is here."

Sympathy for the young woman surfaced. "Are you going to be okay to work the scene?" Gia asked.

The female tech wiped sweat from her brow then seemed to regroup. "Of course. I'll do whatever I can to help catch this demented man."

Murphy handed over the hair and texted the woman the photographs of the scuff marks. Gia did the same with the print. "I also sent this to my partner at the Bureau, so he'll run it for a match. Or at least a partial one."

Murphy's cell buzzed, cutting into the tension-filled air. Gia stiffened, waiting, praying it was good news.

Judging from the grim look on Murphy's face, it wasn't.

She held her breath as he hung up, too afraid to ask.

11:20 A.M., DECEMBER 19, TINLEY

Anxiety knotted every muscle in Murphy's body as he talked to his receptionist. Typically, Tinley was a happy, safe little town. Today they would have been hosting the Christmas parade with floats, music and crafts and games for the children.

Instead the town was virtually on lockdown from the storm, mired in a murder investigation, and searching for a missing resident.

He ended the call, then turned to Gia. "Someone just called in a tip. They spotted a light on in an abandoned barn outside of town. Could be where the CK is holed up."

Hope and fear flickered across her face. "Let's go."

Murphy addressed the crime techs. "Stay here, process the house and make sure no one disturbs the crime scene."

"Copy that," the male agent said.

"I'll transport her body," Dr. Nix murmured.

Murphy thanked them, then he and Gia bundled back up and hurried out to his car. The wind chill had dropped another five degrees since they'd gotten to Sari's. Anyone stranded out in this mess might not survive.

He knew that barn they were about to scope out. It had been abandoned for months, ever since Clyde Owen passed away and the bank had bought his property. With no family, the house had stood empty along with the outbuilding. An investor had bought the land from the bank and already demolished the old fifties ranch.

There was no heat in the barn though. Which meant staying there would be dicey.

Although a desperate killer might take his chances.

"You know where this place is?" Gia asked.

"About three miles outside of town."

They lapsed into silence, the only sound the shrill wind roaring, the heater rumbling, and the defroster struggling to keep the windows clear enough for Murphy to see out. Even with snow tires, he had to drive slowly. Gia huddled deeper inside her coat and rubbed her hands together to keep warm.

"I should have come home to see Carly more often," she mumbled beneath her breath. "But I ...told her I was too busy."

Ahh, hell. Murphy hated the pain and guilt in her voice. Unable to resist, he placed his hand over hers. "You were busy chasing a serial killer, trying to save lives, Gia," he said. "Everyone in the world saw that news story."

"Too busy for my own sister," Gia's voice cracked. "I was always too busy to come back here."

Murphy squeezed her hand. "I'm sure Carly understood."

Her breath gushed out, unsteady and filled with emotions. "She did. But she shouldn't have had to. I've been a terrible sister."

"You are not a terrible sister," Murphy said. "And this isn't your fault. You were trying to stop this maniac."

"And I led him straight to my own family."

Murphy didn't know what to say. Carly had been targeted because Gia was in the limelight. All the reporters had focused on her as the lead investigator in the case.

And she had vowed to nail this killer.

"We're going to get him, Gia," Murphy promised. "Just hang in there."

He wouldn't let her down.

11:20 A.M., DECEMBER 19, TINLEY

Despair threatened as Gia looked out at the frigid weather. If Carly somehow found a way to escape the CK, how would she survive the elements and come back home?

Was she warm? Had he hurt her? "I should have visited more," Gia whispered, a mountain of regret piling on top of her guilt.

"Why didn't you come back?" Murphy asked. "Was it just too hard after your mother died?"

Gia shrugged. "That was part of it. I guess I was a coward. I couldn't stand to be in the house or the store that she loved so much. The memories...they just felt crushing."

"That's understandable," Murphy murmured. "Family is everything."

"It probably seems like I didn't care about mine," Gia said. "Like I'd abandoned Carly."

"You always wanted to leave Tinley," Murphy commented. "I remember in high school, you had high aspirations. There's nothing wrong in that."

Gia gave him a wry look. "I must have sounded snobbish, wanting to leave this town for something bigger and more exciting."

Murphy gripped the steering wheel as he battled the wind force to stay on the road. "It's normal for kids to want to leave the nest and fly on their own. To see the world and what's out there. It takes courage."

"You never left," Gia said softly.

Murphy clenched his jaw. "I thought about it a few times, but the timing was never right."

"What do you mean?"

"My mom," he said. "She was ill. I was all she had. I couldn't just leave her."

Like she'd left Carly.

Gia folded her arms. "That's admirable of you."

"Not really. When my old man started beating me, she stepped in and sent him packing. She was strong back then. I owe her now."

"Oh, Murphy, I didn't know," Gia said, her voice soft. "I'm sorry."

Murphy shrugged. "No big deal." He slanted her an odd look. "And I wasn't criticizing you for leaving, Gia. We had different dreams, that's all. Mine was to have family close and take care of the town. You had to leave Tinley to chase yours."

And to find out what was really important.

He didn't have to say the words. They'd been screaming in her head ever since that terrifying call from Carly.

She wondered what her life would have been like if she'd stayed here and settled down with a man like Murphy. Not seen some of the harsh things she'd seen. Let down her defenses and had a family of her own.

Murphy turned off the main road, and they disappeared into the country, leaving Tinley behind. The fields that were once colorful with rows and rows of corn, now looked desolate, like an icy barren of nothingness.

The sheriff plowed through the snow packed road, the SUV bouncing over ruts and ice. He rounded a corner and drove a couple of miles before the barn slipped into view.

Gia's pulse clamored as she spotted smoke curling into the sky.

The barn was on fire.

CHAPTER NINETEEN

11:45 A.M., December 19, Tinley

THICK SMOKE PLUMES CURLED UPWARD, turning the white fog into a gray blur. Gia threw the car door open, jumped from Murphy's vehicle and jogged toward the barn.

Murphy was right behind her, already on the phone calling the fire department. The smell of burning wood permeated the air, the heat radiating from the fire engulfing her as she neared the barn. Wind howled, feeding the blaze as it whipped through the rotting building.

The fire appeared to be consuming the back of the barn, wood cracking and popping as the blaze ate the old boards.

She pressed her hand to the door to see if it was hot and yanked it away as heat scalded her.

Panic and fear choked her. What if Carly was inside?

She had to save her.

Uncaring what happened to her, she yanked open the door. Murphy yelled at her to stop, but she pulled it hard and it swung open. Flames roared, and suddenly the building exploded. The impact sent her body flying backward, and she collapsed into the snow.

"Dammit, Gia!"

Murphy joined her in a flash, kneeling beside her. "Are you hurt?"

Stars danced in front of her eyes, and an ache throbbed in her shoulder from where she'd hit the ground. The wind bit at her exposed skin, stinging, as she pushed her gloved hands against the frozen ground to get up.

"Gia?"

"I'm okay," she whispered, more irritated than hurt.

Murphy curled his fingers around her arm and helped her up. She swayed slightly and he steadied her.

"I have to see if Carly's inside." She started forward, but Murphy grabbed her and held her back.

"It's too dangerous."

She shoved at his hands, struggling to get free. If her sister was in there, could she still be alive?

"Let me go, Murphy!" She beat at his chest with her fists, but he wrapped his arms around her and held her, absorbing the brunt of her rage and frustration.

"I can't, Gia, it's not safe," he murmured against her ear.

"But Carly might be inside," she cried, tears pouring freely now.

He rubbed slow circles over her back. "I don't think so. Think about it. Fire is not this psycho's MO."

She sobbed out loud. Hysteria was taking over, not logic, her chest heaving.

"You know I'm right," Murphy said gruffly. "He's methodical and plans out his crimes. He likes attention and poses his victims then leaves them, so they'll be found easily."

What he was saying was true. But the terror she'd tried to

keep at bay since that phone call from her sister obliterated rational thought.

"He would not leave Carly here in a fire," Murphy said. "She's more important to him than any of the others because she's your sister. He has to be keeping her somewhere until he's ready to finish his game."

"But where?" Gia cried. "And how? Your men are looking but they have nothing. She could be anywhere. She could even be freezing to death." She pulled away slightly, enough to look at the fire again. "What if was holding her there, and she set the fire to keep warm and it got out of control?"

"Then she would have come out."

Gia wanted to believe him. But her sister could have been too weak to escape?

11:50 A.M., DECEMBER 19, TINLEY

Murphy believed what he'd said. But Gia also had a point.

With the damn blizzard and wind-chill factor plunging, if Carly had been left in that barn, she would have been desperate for heat. She could have somehow set the fire, then the old wood caught, and the flames spread.

A thunderous roar blended with the howling wind. The roof on the barn collapsed, the sides crumbling. Gia gasped, and they both backed up another few feet as heat seared them.

He coaxed her back toward his vehicle. "Get inside and warm up," he said as he opened the passenger door.

"But —"

"The fire is too hot to see or do anything right now. It has to burn out before anyone can go in."

Gia wrapped her arms around herself after she climbed in. She was trembling so badly she looked as if she might shatter into pieces.

He closed the door and walked around to the driver's side. Sliding behind the wheel, he started the engine. The heater burst to life, the windshield fogging over with frost as snow continued to pummel the earth.

Murphy retrieved binoculars from his car, stepped out and walked back toward the barn. In spite of the wind, the heat from the blaze prevented him from getting too close.

But he was anxious himself to know if someone was trapped in that fire.

He aimed the binoculars at the burning barn. The blaze was already dwindling, the wet conditions preventing it from spreading to the nearby trees. He peered through the lenses and scanned the area. Charred wood, straw and debris dotted the snow. A few metal barn tools were piled next to one wall.

Near it, he detected a hump that could be a bale of hay or bag of feed.

Or a body.

His phone buzzed. It was his receptionist, Willa Dean, so he connected. "Sheriff Malone."

"Sheriff, this may not be anything, but Jim from the county office said Harley, the guy who drives the snowplow, hasn't called in in hours. Said he plowed real early, then took a break from the elements but was supposed to go out and do the main road again, then the side roads. Jim's worried something happened to him."

Murphy tugged his jacket hood up over his snow hat. He'd detected snowplow tracks at Sari's. And now Harley was missing.

What if the killer had done something to Harley, and then used the snowplow to reach Sari's place? He could have killed her at her house, then driven away and no one would have suspected a thing.

A fire engine wailed in the distance, and Murphy headed back toward his vehicle. He punched Cody's number as he ducked inside to warm up.

Gia was watching the flames die down, her face tormented.

Murphy checked in with Cody and filled him in. Cody had been busy helping with an accident and a family trapped in their house where the roof had collapsed.

"Keep an eye out for Harley," Murphy told Cody as he hung up.

Gia was watching him. "What was that about the snow-plow driver?"

"I saw snowplow tracks at Sari's. Made me wonder if the perp is using it to get around."

The fire engine careened up the drive and screeched to a halt, and Murphy reached for the door handle. Gia did the same, but he squeezed her hand. "Stay here where it's warm. I'll let you know if they find anything."

If the lump he'd seen in the barn was a body, he wanted to see who it was without alarming Gia.

12:30 P.M., DECEMBER 19, TINLEY

While the fire team worked the scene, Gia thumbed through her photo album on her phone. She had to do something to distract herself.

Tears pricked her eyes. There were dozens of shots she'd saved of her mother and sister when her mother was alive.

But very few of she and Carly in the last three years. All the birthdays and holidays and vacations they could have spent together, and she'd chosen to throw herself into the job chasing killers instead of seeing her precious sister.

She would never forgive herself if she didn't find her and bring her home safely.

Drawing in a deep breath, Gia vowed to make it up to her. From now on, she wouldn't miss a single Christmas, or birthday or holiday.

Her phone buzzed, and she startled, then checked the number. Brantley.

She hit Connect. "Please tell me you have a lead."

His weary sigh made her stomach plummet. "I'm not sure. I finally got through to the airlines. Dr. Whitman booked a flight to Little Rock, but he didn't make the flight. So somewhere between that little town of Tinley and the airport, he disappeared."

"Then he could still be here, hiding out," Gia said.

"True. I've checked all the hotels, motels and inns between the airport and Tinley, and no one by the name of Parker Whitman is registered."

"He may have registered under a fake name."

"Already looking into that," Brantley said. "Our analyst is researching everyone on the registry from all those places, but that's a good number. It'll take some time. He's running background checks on all the males."

"Did you find out anything else about Whitman?"

"The receptionist at his clinic said he was a mystery to her. That one minute he was charming, especially with the female patients. The next minute he was brooding. Took the divorce hard, said that's the reason he was moving."

"Did you talk to the ex?"

"I haven't been able to reach her, but I'll keep trying."

Unease shivered up Gia's spine. Most serial killers started with a personal target, someone who'd triggered their anger and rage. If Whitman's wife couldn't be found, she could have disappeared on her own.

Or she could have been his first victim.

Except he'd left the first ornament attached to Page Gleeson. Not related.

Maybe Page wasn't his first victim though? Killing his wife could have whetted his appetite for murder.

Her phone beeped in with another call, and she told Brantley to keep her posted, then connected.

"Special Agent Franklin, it's Inez at Mistletoe Manor."

"Yes?"

"The sheriff said to call if we saw anyone or anything suspicious, and well, I might have seen something."

"What is it?"

"It's one of the guests," Inez said. "He came in earlier in a rush, and he looked all harried."

Gia drummed her fingers on her leg. "Go on."

"I think he had blood on his clothes."

Her pulse jumped. "Is he still there?"

"Yes, I believe so." Nervous tension tinged the woman's voice. "He ran up the stairs to his room in a hurry, and I haven't seen him since."

"What name did he use to register?"

"Ray Folsom."

"Listen, Inez. If he comes back down, don't let on that you think anything is off or that you called me," Gia said. "I'll be right over."

"Okay. Please hurry. I don't like the thought that that horrible killer might be staying here in my inn."

Neither did she. "Just stay calm. I'm on my way." As soon as she hung up, she texted Brantley the name Ray Folsom and asked him to investigate the guy.

Then she jumped from the vehicle, wrapped her scarf around

her face and trudged through the snow to talk to Murphy. She made it up the hill and had just reached him when she called out his name. He turned to her, but she went bone still.

The firefighters had extinguished what remained of the blaze. And two of them were carrying a body from the ashes.

CHAPTER TWENTY

12:50 P.M., DECEMBER 19, TINLEY

A SENSE of trepidation needled Murphy as he watched the firefighters carry the body from the remains of the barn toward their truck where they'd already laid out a tarp. The corpse was badly burned, clothes charred and skin so black with soot it was unrecognizable.

"Is it … her?" Gia asked in a choked voice.

Murphy was tempted to lie, but Gia was too smart for that. "I don't know, so don't go there yet, Gia. Remember, this is not the killer's MO."

She nodded against him although her body was trembling so badly she thought her legs would buckle. Murphy wrapped his arms around and soothed her with soft words.

She clung to him for a moment, then suddenly straightened and tore away from him. Her boots sank in the snow, and she stumbled. Murphy grabbed her arm and the two of them battled their way toward the body together.

By the time they reached it, one of the firefighters was ending a call. "ME is on his way with a transport vehicle."

Gia stepped closer, but Murphy held her back. "What can you tell about the victim?"

Firefighter Jeremy Rush pushed his helmet up and ran a hand through his sweat soaked hair. Murphy had worked with Jeremy before. In small towns, often people assumed more than one role. Jeremy was trained as an arson investigator. "Nothing much yet. Except the body belongs to a male."

Gia sagged in relief next to him.

Another firefighter gently raked his gloved fingers over the man's charred clothing in search of an ID but shook his head, indicating he hadn't found one.

"Who owned the barn?" Jeremy asked.

"Man named Clyde, but he died two years ago. Farm has been abandoned since."

"Could be a homeless person seeking shelter from the storm," Jeremy suggested. "ME will have to run tests and use dental records to identify him."

Gia straightened, rubbing her arms with her hands to ward off the bitter cold. "Do you know how the fire started or if it was intentional?"

Jeremy shrugged. "Not yet. There was an old propane tank inside along with what looked like some chemicals. We'll do an investigation when we're able to sort through it all."

Gia thanked him, nudged Murphy and explained about the phone call from Inez.

Murphy squared his shoulders. "Can you handle it here and meet the ME?" he asked Jeremy.

"Sure. We have to stay and make sure the fire doesn't start up again anyway, then search for forensics."

Murphy clutched Gia's arm. "Let's go see this Ray Folsom guy."

1:00 P.M., DECEMBER 19, TINLEY

Gia tried to shake the images of the dead man from her mind as Murphy drove toward Mistletoe Inn.

Remembering Murphy's big strong hands holding her, offering her comfort, rejuvenated her courage, and a flood of longing coursed through her, triggering a memory she'd thought lost forever. She and Murphy had gone sledding the winter they'd dated. She'd been thrilled at the ride and at having an excuse to wrap her arms around Murphy's waist and hold on. They'd crashed coming down the hill and were half buried in the snow. But oblivious to the cold he'd helped her up then kissed her.

His SUV skidded slightly, jarring her from the memory. He slowed, his hands gripping the steering wheel to keep the vehicle between the lines. They passed a stranded car that had been abandoned on the side of the road. It had nosedived into the ditch and would have to be hauled out.

He pulled off the road and climbed out to make sure no one was inside. His expression looked grim as he returned to the SUV. "Driver left a note saying they'd called a tow, that a trucker came along and gave him a ride to the inn."

"People are trusting around here, aren't they?" Gia said wistfully. "Although with a killer in town, I don't know why."

"Maybe the driver knew the person who stopped," Murphy suggested. "Besides, what choice did he have? He wouldn't last long stranded out in these temperatures."

"True. It's just different in Florida. I mean people are friendly. But everyone's busy with their lives and families and jobs. It's also a vacation spot, so there are a lot of transients and snowbirds."

"That would make it difficult to make friends," Murphy murmured.

"It does," Gia admitted. "Hard to get invested when you know someone's leaving."

His eyes darkened, a tense second stretching between them. Then Murphy seemed to shake off the awkward moment.

"But you like Florida?"

Gia shrugged. At first when she'd moved to the Sunshine State, she'd enjoyed the warm weather and the anonymity. In Tinley, everyone knew everyone's business.

She hadn't felt the need to get too close to anyone.

She liked being alone.

But now that thought seemed daunting...

Had she immersed herself in her job because she was too afraid to get involved with a man? With Murphy? Too afraid of losing herself?

Too afraid of losing *him*?

Up ahead, the sound of an engine cut into the roar of the wind, and Gia saw a car speeding around the corner toward them. The car driver had lost control and the vehicle flew into a spin.

"Hold on." Murphy swerved to the right to avoid hitting the vehicle head on.

Gia clutched the seat as she was jerked around, then was slammed against the passenger door. The impact wrenched her shoulder. Murphy cursed and held on tight to the wheel in an attempt to keep from crashing.

He scraped the edge of the tree but managed to stay on the road. The other car barreled across the highway and careened toward the embankment. Brakes squealed, and the car slammed into the ditch, the front-bumper crunching.

Murphy veered to the side and parked, then jumped out running. She tugged her scarf around her face, and followed, boots chugging through the snow, her breath coming out in pants as she fought the force of the wind.

By the time she reached the sedan, Murphy was opening the driver's door. Gia made it to the vehicle just as he cleared away the air bag.

A young woman with long dark hair was slumped forward, blood on her forehead and trickling down the side of her face. Murphy pressed two fingers to the woman's neck to check for a pulse. A second later, he gave a little nod that she was alive.

Gia clenched her phone. "I'll call an ambulance."

"It'll be faster if we take her to the hospital."

He raked the woman's hair from her face. "It's Lori Everland from the hair salon." He gently rubbed her back. "Lori, can you hear me? It's Sheriff Malone."

The young woman moaned, then moved her head slightly, opened her eyes and squinted up at Murphy. "What happened?"

"You lost control and had an accident," Murphy said. "Are you okay? Does anything hurt? Your neck? Your legs?"

She appeared disoriented but raised a hand to her temple. Her fingers came away sticky with blood. Glass from the windshield had shattered on impact, and dotted her coat, the seat and floor.

"I'm okay. My chest just hurts."

"The force of the air bag probably bruised your ribs," Murphy said. "If you're okay to move, I'll drive you to the hospital."

The young woman nodded, and Murphy cut away the seat belt, then scooped her into his arms. Gia reached inside and retrieved Lori's purse and phone. Lori groaned but wrapped her arms around Murphy's neck, and Gia and Murphy plowed through the snow back to his SUV.

Gia snagged a blanket from the trunk, along with Murphy's first-aid kit. Murphy settled Lori in the back, and Gia climbed in beside her. Then he crawled in the driver's seat, started the engine and fired up the heater.

Gia pressed a clean gauze strip to the cut on Lori's fore-head then examined it. "The cut doesn't look too deep. But you may need a couple of stitches."

"Thanks," Lori whispered. "I guess it was stupid to be driving in this."

"Why were you?" Gia asked.

The young woman bit her bottom lip. "I heard the report about Sari. Then I heard a banging sound behind my house. The trash can lid bounced across the yard, and the windows rattled. Then I saw a shadow on my deck and heard someone jiggling the doorknob." Her chest heaved. "I got spooked and didn't want to be alone, so I decided to go to my friend's house for the night."

Gia patted her arm. "Well, you're safe now." Except she'd panicked.

Or had she?

Had the killer decided to sneak inside her place to ride out the weather? Or had he planned to take Lori as his next victim?

1:30 P.M., DECEMBER 19, TINLEY

Murphy pulled up to the hospital ER and parked, his gut churning. It had taken him almost half an hour to drive the seven miles to the hospital.

Thank God Lori hadn't been seriously injured.

Admiration for Gia mounted. In spite of the fact that she was terrified for her sister and on the hunt for a serial killer, she'd comforted the other woman and kept a level head.

Hospital attendees met them at the entrance to the ER.

"Is there anyone you need me to call?" Murphy asked as they helped Lori into a wheelchair.

"My sister, Peggy," Lori said.

Murphy got the number from her, then called and explained the situation to Peggy while Gia accompanied Lori into the ER. Peggy was frantic and insisted she'd come as soon as she could get out in the weather to make it there.

Murphy went inside to tell Lori, and saw Gia standing by her bed soothing the woman's fears. The lights flicked off, then on again, and Murphy's chest clenched. Soon the entire town might be in the dark.

In the dark with a serial killer on the loose and panic rising.

CHAPTER TWENTY-ONE

2:00 P.M., December 19, Tinley

GIA HAD to step out of the ER room while Lori assured Peggy not to worry. The love in Lori's voice for her older sister mirrored the sweet adoration she'd always received from Carly.

Adoration she hadn't always deserved.

She splashed cold water on her face in the ladies' room, blinking to stem the tears, then stared at herself in the mirror.

If Carly dies, it's your fault.

The thought of not seeing her sister again, not decorating the tree and roasting marshmallows and drinking wine while they listened to Christmas carols made tears clog her throat.

I'll make it up to you, sis, just hang in there.

A knock sounded at the door. "Gia, are you okay?"

No, hell, no she wasn't. But she dried her face, pasted on her professional mask and stepped outside. She'd never been a quitter. Although she had wrapped herself in her own grief after their mother passed and left Carly alone.

She didn't intend to run away again, or to quit on her sister.

"I'm fine," she said, grateful Murphy didn't acknowledge the warble in her voice.

"Let's go to the inn before they lose power, too."

She buttoned her coat, secured her weapon in her pocket, then followed the sheriff through the ER and outside into the parking lot.

The sky was darkening now, the thick snow clouds shrouding the light and casting a gray glow across the land. She climbed in the car and buckled her seatbelt, then checked her phone.

Nothing from Brantley yet.

High velocity winds and icy roads forced Murphy to crawl toward the B & B. Thankfully, most people were heeding the warnings to stay tucked inside. The decorations on the storefronts were already battered and torn from the wind, the street becoming almost impassable.

He finally veered into the drive for the Mistletoe Inn. The normally cheerful place looked haunted with gray skies casting shadows all around the property. Lights from the Christmas tree inside fought to be seen through the frosted windowpanes.

Several cars were parked in the small lot, half buried now in snow and debris blown in by the storm.

Murphy parked and they hurried up the sidewalk to the front porch. As they entered, the seven-foot Douglas-fir tree was a bright spot in a dismal day. Christmas lights draped the door and holiday artwork adorned the walls of the keeping room/breakfast area to the right. Inez served breakfast and lunch, but dinner was on your own. She even offered wine and cheese and crackers daily at five for social hour, bringing guests together to chat and relax before the evening festivities.

A fire roared from the brick fireplace where guests had gathered to stay warm. Tables and comfy chairs in the adjoining room offered seating for meals, reading nooks, and also served as space for families to gather for board games. A family was there now intent in a game of Monopoly. A teenage boy and girl sat sullen at another table. "This is the worst Christmas ever," the boy grumbled.

"We don't even have internet here," the girl complained as she gestured to her phone.

The mother looked harried. "We can't help it that the weather canceled the festival."

Voices rumbled from two chairs flanking the fireplace and drifted toward Gia, and she spotted two young women hunkered together. "I wish we could get out of town. That crazy serial killer just murdered a local girl."

"I know, it's so scary. She was our age. What if he tries to kidnap us?"

"I guess we have to stay locked in here just to be safe," the first girl whispered.

Gia grimaced. The panic was mounting. It would only grow worse in the next forty-eight hours.

2:25 P.M., DECEMBER 19, TINLEY

Murphy walked straight to the front desk. "Hey, Inez. Is that Folsom guy still here?"

Inez glanced over his shoulder as if searching for the man. "I haven't seen him come down yet. He's driving a dark green Pathfinder. Did you see it in the lot?"

Murphy stepped to the side window that overlooked the parking lot. "It's still there."

Gia joined him. "Let's gather all the guests down here for questioning. That way he won't feel singled out, get spooked and run."

"Good idea," Murphy agreed. "Inez, do you mind going door to door and asking the guests to meet us in the common room?"

"Sure."

"How many guests are there?" Gia asked.

"We have twenty rooms and they're all full."

"How many single men?" she asked.

Inez shook her head. "None."

"What about Ray Folsom?"

She checked the register. "He registered as Mr. and Mrs. Folsom. Although I've yet to see the wife."

Gia drummed her fingers on the counter. "I'll accompany you to the rooms in case Folsom reacts."

Murphy removed his snow hat and stuffed it into his pocket. "I'll keep watch in case he comes down the back stairwell and tries to leave."

While Gia and Inez disappeared down the hall to find Folsom, a few families wandered in. Murphy quickly questioned and dismissed them, keeping an eye out for Folsom.

A few minutes later, he thought he spotted him come down the stairs. A barrel-chested guy with wiry hair wearing a t-shirt emblazoned with a hunting logo. The man's eyes kept darting sideways across the room as if he was scouting out an escape route.

Concerned voices rumbled through the group. "Is the storm getting worse?" one of the men asked.

"How long will be snowed in?"

"Are we losing power?"

"When will they clear the roads so we can leave?"

Murphy raised a hand to quiet them. "Holly is bearing down on us now. At the rate it's passing through, it'll move on quickly, but who knows how long the airport will be shut down, and it'll take days to dig ourselves out. But the state is sending help, so try to remain calm."

"How can we stay calm when a serial killer is stalking women here?" a young woman in her twenties asked. "When he killed that nice girl who ran the sweet shop?"

"The owner of the Christmas shop was kidnapped, too," another girl screeched.

More voices rumbled, tones panicked and full of fear.

"What are you doing to find him?" A man with silver hair asked.

Murphy shifted. "Search crews are looking for the missing woman, and law enforcement is on high alert." He scanned the room, scrutinizing the group. They had a right to be nervous because of the weather and the serial killer.

But he was looking for more than a case of nerves.

His phone buzzed with a text. Dr. Nix from the ME's office. "Identified man pulled from the barn fire. It's Harley. Gunshot wound to the chest. He was dead before the fire ever started."

Murphy clenched his jaw. Dammit. Tinley had just lost another one of their own. And the fire was definitely set to cover his murder.

Inez said Folsom had blood on his clothes. The man in the hunting shirt would know how to use a gun.

That blood could belong to Harley.

2:45 P.M., DECEMBER 19, TINLEY

Gia introduced herself and explained they ~~were simply~~ conducting routine questioning, looking for anyone who might have seen something, that any detail might help. "Get comfortable, folks and be patient. Inez will serve refreshments while you wait."

Unease rippled through the group, but the innkeeper brought cookies, coffee, tea and lemonade for the bar area, and the guests accepted the inevitable.

Murphy started pulling individuals, starting with the females, and talking to them at a table near the front of the room. A strategic move so he could stand guard if someone tried to escape.

Gia situated herself at a table on the opposite side nearer the rear exit. They spent the next half hour asking guests general questions about when they'd arrived, if they'd seen anyone or anything suspicious, and eliminating families.

The couples were easy. With the storm forcing them to stay inside, they alibied each other. Most guests had arrived a couple of days earlier and enjoyed gift shopping before the festivities were scheduled to begin. Three of the women remembered meeting Carly in *Happy Holidays!* and offered Gia their sympathies. Two others had met Sari and were visibly upset over her death.

With the couples and females eliminated, and no single men registered at the inn, Gia headed toward the coffee bar where she'd seen Ray Folsom. His turn now.

But he was gone.

Gritting her jaw, she stepped to the window to look at the parking lot and saw him hurrying through the snow to that green Pathfinder.

Instincts kicked in, and she gestured to Murphy that Folsom was outside. Yanking on their coats, they headed in opposite directions. Murphy took the front door while she exited the back. Wind hurled debris and leaves across the pristine white, slashing thin limbs and sending them thrashing to the ground.

She dodged a couple of branches and made it to the man just as he reached his car.

"Stop, Mr. Folsom. Police."

He froze, then angled his big burly body toward her, dark eyes flashing with irritation.

"We need to talk," Gia said. "Come back inside."

"I didn't do anything wrong," he bellowed, then he jerked open the car door.

Gia grabbed his arm in an attempt to pull him away, but he turned and shoved her as hard as he could. She staggered backward and scrambled to stay on her feet but failed.

Before she could retrieve her gun, Murphy's loud voice barked from behind her. "You just assaulted a federal agent, Mr. Folsom. Now, if you know what's good for you, you'll put your hands up and step away from the vehicle."

Folsom's big body froze, and he slowly lifted his hands in surrender. Gia silently cursed herself for letting him get the better of her and pushed to her feet.

Murphy aimed her a sideways look. "You okay?"

"Yeah," she muttered, her pride smarting.

Murphy yanked the man's hands behind him and hand-cuffed him.

"I didn't do anything, she attacked me!" Folsom shouted.

Gia took one glance into the interior of his car and spotted blood. A lot of it.

Anger slammed into her. She closed the distance between them and stared into the man's dark gray eyes, her hand clenching her gun as she aimed it at his chest.

"Where's my sister?" she growled. "Where is she?"

CHAPTER TWENTY-TWO

3:00 P.M., December 19, Tinley

MURPHY PLACED a hand on Gia's back. "Let's take him in for questioning. We have to do this by the book."

Gia glared at him, but reluctantly stepped away. Murphy gripped Folsom's arm and shoved him toward his police car. The commotion had drawn several guests, fear and panic on the people's faces. Then the questions began.

"What's going on?"

"Is he this serial killer?"

"Are we in danger?"

Gia quickly hurried over to calm them. "Everything's fine, folks. And you're safe. Go back inside and stay there. We're just taking Mr. Folsom in for questioning. But the weather is growing worse by the minute. Stay tucked in and warm."

Inez looked rattled but began consoling the frightened guests. "We'll have drinks and movie night in a bit. But first maybe we can make Christmas cookies, then I have arts and crafts supplies so we can make Christmas decorations with the children."

Her reassurance along with the bitter wind sent the people scurrying back inside. Hopefully Inez could restore some of the Christmas spirit the weather and serial killer were destroying.

It would definitely be a holiday to remember. But not in a good way.

Gia joined Murphy at the car, while Folsom protested from the back seat.

"There's blood in his vehicle," Gia said with a dark scowl.

"I'll get my kit and take a sample. Stay here with Folsom."

Gia murmured she would, and he retrieved his kit from the back of his SUV and carried it over to the Pathfinder. First, he snapped pictures of the interior and exterior, then tested a sample to determine if the stain on the back seat was blood.

It tested positive.

Carly had been cut grabbing the ornaments in her shop when she'd been abducted. Was this her blood?

He shined a light across the interior searching for other forensics and found some short hair fibers. Not Carly's. Her hair was long and blonde.

These fibers were coarse, too. Maybe an animal's?

He collected and bagged them, then picked up a small button that looked as if it had been ripped from a woman's blouse.

Satisfied that he had enough, at least to question Folsom, he walked back to the inn and asked Inez to tell her handyman who stayed on the property to make sure no one touched the vehicle. He considered roping it off with crime tape, but at this point, he had no idea if it was a crime scene or not.

Then he went to search Folsom's room. A small suitcase

sat on the luggage rack in the corner. Gloves intact, he rifled through the suitcase and found two pairs of jeans, three flannel shirts, underwear, and socks.

He moved to the dresser and searched it, but the drawers were empty. So was the desk. A pair of khaki slacks and a button-down collared shirt hung in the closet. Not the button he was looking for though.

Murphy checked the bathroom next. Basic toiletries. And then...bloody clothes on the floor.

His pulse hammered. Did the blood belong to Folsom? Or to Carly? His theory about her cutting herself on the ornaments fit. Unless Folsom had cut himself on the ornaments?

He found a plastic laundry bag in the closet and put the bloody clothes inside. Although the bad weather would impede getting the evidence he'd collected to a lab.

It would also take time to process it when he did get it there.

Maybe he could use the items to wrangle a confession from the man.

He scratched his head. Although if Folsom was the CK, where was the box of ornaments?

He hadn't found them in Folsom's car.

He searched the bathroom cabinet, then checked under the bed and the top shelf of the closet. Nothing. Then the safe.

Empty.

Dammit.

Knowing Gia was waiting, and they needed to question Folsom, Murphy locked the room, went down the steps and gave Inez the key. "Please don't clean in there. I may want a crime team to process it."

"Did you find something?" Inez asked, wide-eyed.

"Some bloody clothes," Murphy admitted. "Don't let anyone in that room except the crime investigators."

She fidgeted with the register on the desk. "All right. Are you arresting him?"

Murphy shrugged. "Yes, for assaulting a federal agent. I also want to hold him for questioning."

She lifted a shaky hand to her heart. "Good. That man made me nervous."

Grim-faced, Murphy carried the bag of clothes outside. Gia had slipped into his SUV and had the engine running to stay warm. When Murphy climbed in, Folsom sat sullen-faced and silent.

Gia folded her arms. "He claims the blood in his car was from a deer that he hit it on his way back to the inn. Said he stained his clothes dragging the deer off the highway."

"I didn't want anyone else to hit it and have an accident," Folsom snapped.

"Did you put it in a refrigerator in someone's house?" Murphy asked.

Folsom's eyebrows climbed his forehead. "What? No, I told you I dragged it back into the woods."

His story could be true. The short coarse hairs could be deer hair.

But if there was any possibility Folsom had abducted Carly, Murphy couldn't turn the man loose.

Besides, they'd caught Folsom running.

That made him look guilty as sin.

3:10 P.M., DECEMBER 19, TINLEY

Gia confiscated Folsom's phone and searched through it, looking at his contacts and phone history.

She thought he might have phoned her sister at the shop or home but didn't see either number. She searched for area codes for Delray Beach, Savannah and Gulf Shores. A Florida area code popped up.

She texted Brantley that Folsom was in custody and to send her anything he'd dug up on the man.

Waiting was painful though. She flexed her hands in an effort to maintain self-control. She wanted to pound the man until he confessed where he was holding her sister. And if that blood in his car belonged to Carly.

But her interrogation training kicked in, and she forced herself to remain calm as Murphy maneuvered the vehicle to the police station. Folsom was still grumbling that he hadn't done anything wrong when Murphy put him in an interrogation room. With a grunt, Folsom dropped into the metal chair that was bolted to the floor.

Instead of taking the seat across from him, Gia moved a chair directly in front of him, facing him. She was so close their knees almost touched. Creating a more intimate feeling and invading his personal space was a technique she'd learned from an expert FBI interrogator who taught nationwide.

If she came at Folsom too hard, he'd shut down and lawyer up, and she'd lose her chance at extracting information.

Murphy offered Folsom a bottle of water, and the man guzzled it as if he was dehydrated. Nerves made people sweat.

Folsom was sweating profusely. He also averted his eyes and jiggled his leg up and down.

He's hiding something.

Liars squirmed and backed away when the interrogator became too close.

Murphy narrowed his eyes in question, but she gestured to let her have a go at him first.

"Mr. Folsom, do you know who I am?" She watched carefully for his reaction.

He lifted his shoulders in a shrug. "Of course. Everyone knows who you are. You've been all over the news."

"True. I also grew up here in Tinley." She gave him a small smile. "What about you? Where are you from?"

"Originally from Louisiana."

"I've been to New Orleans a few times. It's a cool town."

A small smile tugged at the corner of his mouth as if he was reliving a fun memory. "Crazy during Mardi Gras."

"What part of New Orleans did you live in?"

"Terrytown, across the bridge."

"Is that where you live now?"

He shifted, relaxed slightly. "Left after Katrina. Wife transferred for her job."

"Where did you move to?"

He looked away, his breathing growing more rapid.

"Mr. Folsom?"

"Florida."

Perfect segue. "Florida." Where the murders began. "What part of Florida?"

"Fort Lauderdale."

Close to Delray Beach. "Do you like it there?"

"No, it's hot as hell."

"How about your wife? Does she like it?"

He started the leg jiggling again. "Yeah, I guess. We don't talk that much anymore."

Gia narrowed her eyes. "I don't understand."

"We're separated," he said, a trace of bitterness in his voice. "I lost my job last year, and she up and left."

"You wanted to make your marriage work?"

He scratched his chest. "I did. She always loved Christmas and saw an article about this town being crazy over it. I bought us tickets to come for the festival hoping to win her back."

Gia raised a brow. "Then she came with you?"

"No. Said she'd think about it and maybe meet me here." Anger flared in the man's eyes, then he glanced down at his hands. His fingernails were still stained with what appeared to be dried blood.

Then he reached for the water bottle and took a long swallow again. Water trickled down the side of his face, and he swiped at it with the back of his hand. "She didn't make it, though. I reckon her flight got cancelled because of this freak storm."

Gia cut a sideways look toward Murphy, silently telling him to check out the man's story. Inez said he registered as Mr. and Mrs. Folsom. Had his wife planned to come and been unable to because of the weather? Or was he lying?

"But you arrived all right."

Folsom shifted, then pinned her with narrowed eyes. "I had an early flight. But you don't really care about my marriage and my wife now, do you?"

Oh, yes, she did. The timing might be important. If the woman had left him right before Christmas, it could have triggered his rage.

Then he'd started killing as his way of revenge against his wife.

3:30 P.M., DECEMBER 19, TINLEY

Murphy clenched his jaw as he hung up the phone. The police department in Ft. Lauderdale had been extremely helpful. When he explained he had a suspect in his jail that potentially could be the Christmas Killer, their lead detective jumped on the line.

They found Folsom's home address, as well as his wife's, and were sending officers to check both properties. Their preliminary background check showed that Folsom's wife served him with divorce papers December 2nd.

The timing could be significant.

She'd also filed a restraining order against him, claiming he'd tried to choke her when she said she was leaving him.

The Christmas Killer had strangled his victims.

The detective was going to explore whether or not Mrs. Folsom had tried to make a flight to Nebraska, or if she was ever even issued a ticket.

Even more interesting, Folsom drove a big truck for a large retail store that delivered all across the U.S.

Murphy strode back to the interrogation room, armed with information, and the forensics he'd recovered from the room.

Although Gia appeared calm, a slight tightening of her jaw indicated she was anything but relaxed.

Every hour her sister was missing had to be excruciating. He was surprised she'd held herself together this long. More than anything he wanted to ease her pain and make things right for her again.

"Mr. Folsom," Murphy said, his voice hard. "You have some explaining to do."

The man instantly stiffened, rocking his chair back slightly then letting the chair legs hit the floor with a thud.

Murphy dropped the bag of bloody clothes on the table. "I found these in the bathroom of your room at the inn. Looks like a lot of blood."

Folsom's mouth thinned into a tight line. "I already told *her*," he spat the word out as if it was a bad word, "I hit a deer and dragged it off the road. That's how my clothes got bloody." He leaned forward as if to stand. "Now can I go?"

Murphy stepped closer. "Not yet. Sit down." He gestured toward the button and the hair he'd collected. "I also found those in your car."

Folsom looked confused.

"The hair, whose is it?" Murphy asked.

"Probably that stupid deer's," he growled. "Last time I try to do a good deed. Being humane, and now I'm treated like dirt by the cops."

"The button," Murphy pointed out. "It looks as if it came from a woman's blouse."

"I don't know anything about a button," Folsom said. "Maybe you planted it there to set me up."

"Why would I want to set you up?" Murphy asked.

"Because you're a crappy sheriff and someone got killed in your town and you want to pin it on someone, so you'll look like a hero."

Murphy arched a brow. "But if I did that, then the real killer would still be on the loose. And that's dangerous for the women in my town."

Folsom ran a hand over his face and cursed. "I can't believe this. I came here for a vacation because this town was supposed to be friendly and the people make the holidays special, but it's been nothing but a nightmare!"

Clearly the man was disgruntled. Murphy was determined to use that to his advantage.

"Your wife didn't just leave you, did she?" he asked point-edly. "She filed a protective order against you."

Surprised interest made Gia straighten.

"That was a mistake," he said. "She was just mad at the time."

Murphy gave him a deadpan look. Guilty or not, he didn't like this guy. Any man who would hurt a woman deserved to be locked up. "Mad because you tried to strangle her?"

CHAPTER TWENTY-THREE

3:45 P.M., December 19, Tinley

Gia curled her fingers around the edge of the chair seat to keep from grabbing Folsom and shaking him until he confessed the truth.

"I didn't try to strangle her. She lied about that to make me look bad," he snarled.

"Really?" Murphy muttered a sound of disgust. "The judge wouldn't have granted the protective order unless there was some basis to her accusation."

"Oh, she can put on a sweet, innocent act," he said. "Fools everyone into thinking she's a saint when she's a lying, cheating whore."

"Yet you planned this trip to win her back," Gia cut in.

Folsom clenched his jaw, then looked away again.

"You said your wife loved Christmas," Gia said, changing tactics. "Did she decorate a lot?"

Folsom's gaze jerked back to hers as if confused by the

abrupt change in topic. "She did. Strung tinsel and lights everywhere and loved buying ornaments."

Gia jumped on his comment. "Like the Twelve Days of Christmas ornaments? Did she like those?"

The realization of where she was headed dawned in his eyes. "She had all kinds. Bought a new one every year. Liked to collect them from different cities when we took trips."

Gia nodded thoughtfully. "Were ornaments part of your tradition? Or maybe you gave lavish gifts each day?"

Anger flashed on Folsom's face, but he remained silent.

"Is it true that you drive a delivery truck for a living?" Murphy asked.

Folsom's brows furrowed. "Yeah. Been doing it for years."

"And you deliver across the U.S., including Florida, Georgia and Alabama?"

"So?"

"Those were the states where the Christmas Killer has struck," Gia pointed out.

"And then you came here." Murphy pulled crime scene photos of Sari's murder and laid them on the table. "See that ornament? Did you strangle this young woman and tie it to her wrist?"

Folsom's eyes flared with panic. "I don't even know her. Why would I kill her?"

The fact that he didn't automatically deny the charge raised Gia's suspicions.

"Because you were angry at your wife for leaving you," she pointed out. "So angry that once she filed the protective order, you transferred that rage to all women."

"Only a crazy person would do that," Folsom bellowed.

Murphy spread out photos of all the dead girls, starting with the first and lining them up in order according to the days associated with the ornaments.

"Or someone who'd been hurt." Gia strove to sound

sympathetic. "Someone who felt betrayed by their loved one like you did."

Folsom's leg jiggled again.

Murphy tapped the first photograph. "This is Page Gleeson. She was twenty-seven-years old, single, a barista at a coffee shop a block from the boardwalk at Delray Beach. Is that where you met her?"

Folsom scooted back in his chair as if he couldn't tolerate the gruesome sight in the photograph.

"Everyone who worked at the coffee shop with her said she was friendly to the customers," Murphy continued. "Did she wait on you?"

Folsom slanted his eyes toward Gia. "I never met her or any of these other women."

"Really? This is victim two, Kittie Preston," Murphy said. "She was twenty-four, a salesclerk at a shoe store at the mall. You may have bought shoes from her or perhaps you just stood back and watched her. Stalked her until she left the mall after her shift ended."

Sweat trickled down the side of Folsom's face.

Murphy continued, tapping each girl and naming her.

"Victim three, Anita Henderson, owned a food truck. Then the Savannah victims. Avery Wong was only twenty-one and was on vacation with her girlfriends. You may have seen her at the bar where her friends hung out."

Murphy moved on. "This is victim five. Lucy Crandall. She sold t-shirts and souvenirs at a small shop on River Street."

"I told you, I don't know any of these women," Folsom said between clenched teeth.

"You didn't take the time to get to know them," Gia interjected. "You just snuck up on them and snatched them, then choked them."

"I did not!" Folsom bolted up from his seat, causing his chair to clatter onto the floor.

Murphy stepped toward him, a feral look in his eyes. "Sit down, Mr. Folsom."

They stared at each other for a long minute, then Folsom dropped back into the chair with an angry hiss.

Murphy tapped the next pictures in rapid succession. "Victim six, Ruthie Pickley, a waitress at the Crab Hut. Now we move onto Gulf Shores.

"Victim seven, Sissy Wiggins, cleaned rooms at the Motel Five. Victim eight, Marcia Sanchez, worked at a donut shop on the strip by the beach. Victim nine, Terry Ann Igley, owned a pet grooming and boarding service that catered to tourists."

Murphy gestured toward the picture of Sari. "And then you came to Tinley and took Sari."

"Because of me." Gia leaned forward again, pressing her knees against the man's to invade his space again. "You strangled Sari and left her in her house after you abducted my sister. The game is over now, Mr. Folsom." She slammed her hand on the table beside them. "Now tell me where Carly is."

3:55 P.M., DECEMBER 19, TINLEY

Murphy watched Folsom shut down.

"I want a lawyer," the man said. "And when he arrives, I'm going to file charges against you two for false arrest and harassment."

"Just tell me where she is," Gia said, her tone sharper this time. "Sparing her might help you in court."

"A lawyer," Folsom repeated.

Gia stared at the man for a long, painful minute, then stood and paced to the door.

"She's right," Murphy said. "Cooperate and save Carly Franklin, and it'll work in your favor."

"I said I want a lawyer. And I'm not answering any more questions until I speak to one."

Murphy wished to hell he had lab analysis back, something more incriminating he could use against the man. If he'd just found those damn ornaments...

Gia turned back to face him from the doorway. "It'll take time for a lawyer to get here."

"She's right again," Murphy said. "Everything's shutting down, and the roads may be impassable soon."

"Then let me go," Folsom said.

"No way." Murphy stood his ground. "You assaulted a federal agent, remember? And I still believe you're hiding something."

A night in a cell would make the man talk.

If he was the CK and Carly was still alive, she'd be safer with him in jail. Provided he hadn't left her someplace where she'd freeze to death.

"Give me my phone call," Folsom ordered.

Gia breathed out, frustration evident in the sound. Murphy had confiscated the man's phone when he'd first brought Folsom in. He stepped from the room to retrieve it, then returned a minute later and handed it to Folsom.

Folsom's lawyer didn't answer, so he left him a message.

When Folsom finished, Murphy confiscated the phone again. "Come on, I'll show you to your accommodations for the night."

The man's cold stare was lethal. Murphy ignored it and escorted him through the double doors then down a hall to a holding cell.

Gia followed, silent and steaming. Murphy slammed the

cell door shut and locked it. "Let me know when you're ready to talk."

Folsom clenched the bars in a white knuckled grip. "You're going to be sorry for this."

Gia elbowed Murphy aside and pushed her face into Folsom's. "So will you. If you hurt one hair on my sister's head, I'll make you suffer. Then I'll put a bullet in your brain."

Folsom reached out as if to grab her, but Gia stepped back just before his fingers connected with her throat.

4:10 P.M., DECEMBER 19, TINLEY

Gia leaned against the wall in the hall leading to the front of the sheriff's office. She was so mad she was shaking.

Typically, she was good at reading people. But she was on the fence as to whether or not she believed Folsom.

She didn't like him, that much she knew. He was a jerk. Probably deserved for his wife to leave him. But ...but had he abducted Carly and killed ten other young women?

That kind of cold-blooded, methodical murder indicated a psychopath. Folsom was a hothead. His reaction had been volatile. He hadn't even attempted to disguise his emotions.

Serial killers, were often cool, smooth-talking, masters at manipulation who were adept at hiding their inner depravity. They blended into a crowd, looked normal, charmed their victims into trusting them.

Their true colors surfaced in private.

They also got off on looking at crime scene photos or watching the police work a crime scene. It enabled them to relive the thrill of the kill. Playing cat and mouse with the police heightened the pleasure.

Folsom appeared to be none of those things. He exhibited

a lack of self-control, which fit with a spontaneous murder born of rage, not a well-planned out one.

Or a dozen well-planned ones.

With his temper and knee jerk reaction, he would have made mistakes. Left evidence behind. Like the hair in his car and the bloody clothing.

Unless...he was telling the truth, and he'd had no reason to try to hide those things.

"You okay?" Murphy's deep voice interrupted her thoughts.

Gia opened her eyes, but she barely saw Murphy. Instead the images from the crime scene photos flashed like a montage behind her eyes. All those pretty young women dead.

Her sister...

"Breathe." Murphy slowly rubbed her arms. "Deep breaths, Gia."

She leaned into him, pressed her head against his body and soaked up his comforting tone. When she looked up at him, she was calmer, knew she had an ally. A friend.

Maybe more. Someday.

"Time may be running out," she said in a raw whisper. "I have to do something."

Frustration darkened Murphy's angular face. "A few hours in that cell may change his mind about talking."

"If he's our guy," Gia said. "Those damn ornaments are bothering me."

Before the sheriff could respond, Gia's cell phone buzzed. She quickly glanced at it and connected. "Brantley, please tell me you have something."

"I do," Brantley said. "Not sure if it's what you want to hear though."

Fear lodged in her throat. "Just give it to me straight. You have something on Folsom?"

"Not really. His boss at the trucking company said he was a good worker, although he'd seemed off these last few months. Thought he might have been drinking too much because of problems with his wife."

Gia sighed. "Anything else?"

"Just heard from the State Patrol. They found Dr. Whitman."

"What? Where is he? Is he in custody?"

"He had an accident not too far from the airport. His car wound up off the road in a remote section of farmland, crashed into some cornfields. They think it was weather-related."

"Is he okay?" Gia asked.

"Unconscious. Took him to the ER with a head injury, swelling in the brain. Doctors put him in a medically induced coma until the swelling decreases."

"When did this happen?"

"The day he was supposed to fly out. Looks like he crashed on the way to the airport. That's the reason he never made his flight."

Gia's mind raced. "Which means he couldn't have killed Sari Benedict."

Brantley muttered agreement, and Gia pressed her hand to her mouth to stifle a cry.

"I'll keep digging on Folsom," Brantley promised. "I also have a team reviewing security cameras near the locations where all the women were abducted. Maybe we missed something."

"Maybe. Have them pull photos taken at the crime scenes, too. Find out which reporters were there. Maybe they have their own shots and captured the killer hanging around to watch the aftershock of what he'd done."

"On it."

Gia hung up, a sick feeling in the pit of her stomach.

"What's going on?" Murphy asked quietly.

She relayed her partner's information. "If Folsom is innocent, and Dr. Whitman is off the suspect list, we have nothing. No leads." Despair made her voice crack.

Murphy pulled her to him. "We'll find her," he said vehemently.

Gia choked back tears. and he cupped her face between his hands. Their gazes locked. Words unspoken. Tension and his compassion riveted her to his rugged, strong face.

It had been a long time since she'd allowed herself to be comforted, especially by a man. After her mother died, she'd shut down. Closed herself off from others.

Even her sister.

If she lost her now, she would have nobody.

Hungry for his comfort, she pressed her lips to his. For a moment, he went so still she feared he'd push her away. Then he slowly, gently moved his lips over hers. Brushing hers with such tenderness that her heart swelled with longing.

The kiss lasted only a few seconds. It was enough. At least for the moment.

She pulled her lips from his and exhaled. She had to do something. Act. "I want to talk to that reporter." She couldn't just sit around and wait for the killer to take Carly from her. Or for him to strike again.

He'd come to Nebraska because of her. To taunt her. To hurt her.

It was time she gave him what he wanted.

CHAPTER TWENTY-FOUR

4:30 P.M., December 19, Tinley

MURPHY SENSED Gia was about to break. He wanted to bring her sister back to her more than he'd ever wanted anything in his life.

But if he couldn't...

He'd be there when she fell, that is, if she'd let him.

The woman had always been independent.

He massaged her back, wanting to kiss her again. But his phone buzzed, and he forced himself to answer it.

His deputy. "Yeah?"

"Still no sign of Carly," Cody said, anger and worry tingeing his voice. "But there's a ten-car pile-up on the highway. In spite of the storm warnings, folks were panicked because of this case and decided to leave town."

Murphy muttered a curse. "I can't make it there, Sherriff," Cody said. "The road between the cottages and the highway where the accident happened is completely blocked with fallen trees and downed power lines."

He would have to go. "Injuries? Fatalities?"

"Injuries, yes. Don't know about fatalities. Someone called 911. First responders have been notified."

At some point they would be forced to stop responding for their own safety. "I'm on my way. Did you check out all the guests at the cottages?"

"Yeah. Mostly families. One single young woman writing a travel blog who came for the festival and was alone. Another woman in her forties, also alone, who came to look at property. The two of them are going to hang together until this is over. Owner of the cottages said he had another building he planned to renovate for functions like weddings and family reunions. I'm going there now."

Murphy thanked him and hung up, then filled Gia in on what was going on.

"Good grief, people are driving in this weather because they're scared."

"I know. Not smart." He was surprised they hadn't started fleeing town the moment word spread the CK had struck in Tinley.

"I have to go."

Gia nodded. "I'll come with you."

Murphy gently touched her arm. "Why don't you stay and try to rest a little bit?"

"I can't rest until I find Carly."

4:45 P.M., DECEMBER 19, TINLEY

Just the thought of closing her eyes brought images of the Christmas tree waiting for she and Carly to decorate. There were no packages under the tree either, not like when they were little. Although gifts didn't matter.

The only thing she wanted was her sister home.

Nostalgia washed over Gia. Even though their mother had been on a tight budget, she used to wrap small presents so they could open one each day of the month. She and Carly saved up their allowances and went to the discount store and bought presents for each other. One year they'd bought each other the same set of paper dolls without realizing it. Another year, Carly had given her a bracelet making kit and she had given Carly a different jewelry set. They'd spent the entire day making friendship bracelets and pretty necklaces for each other.

Their mother had turned wrapping presents into a party. Mountains of tissue, holiday wrapping paper and gift bags would be spread all over the den. Her mother hadn't minded the mess. Instead, she'd laughed and started a tissue paper fight.

She'd made everything so special.

Gia missed her so much she could barely breathe.

She couldn't lose her sister. They would be together again. She couldn't imagine the outcome any differently.

"I might be able to help," Gia said. "Besides, maybe one of those people panicked because they saw something."

Murphy looked grim, but he motioned okay. He'd been such a rock for her that she wanted to help him. The bitter blast of wind stung her cheeks as they hurried outside to his vehicle. The siren on his police vehicle wailed as he drove onto the icy road.

The snow was turning into whiteout conditions. Murphy powered up the defroster and wipers, but they screeched across the frosted glass as they struggled to clear it and were failing miserably.

How were they going to find Carly in this disaster? Was the CK already choosing his last victim?

An ambulance and fire engine roared up at the same time

they did. The pile-up was bad. Ten cars, crashed in all different directions across the highway, some in the ditches, one crunched between two trees, another upside down. Two others were half buried in the snow.

She, Murphy, and the rescue workers jumped into motion, hurrying from car to car to assess injuries. The next half hour was chaos as they helped people from their vehicles and the paramedics examined them. Most had sustained only minor injuries, bruises and cuts, but one man had a broken arm, and another woman was complaining of severe leg pain. Firefighters also worked to rescue a young couple trapped in their small sedan.

Murphy called for back-up ambulances and phoned the preacher at the local church. He agreed to send parishioners with vans to transport victims to the hospital.

Clarissa Klondike, the local news reporter, arrived with a camera team to capture the chaos. Murphy took statements from the drivers to figure out what exactly had happened. Weather definitely played a part.

So did fear and panic.

Although most of the folks involved in the accident didn't fit the profile for the CK's victims, gossip about the snow-plow driver's death had leaked, and they were terrified of being caught up in the maniac's clutches as they thought Harley had.

No one had seen anything suspicious though. If they had, how would they know? Everyone was bundled up in heavy winter clothing, scarves, hats and gloves, making them indistinguishable. Stores were closed and people were locked inside, not out in town where they might encounter the CK.

Of if they had, he'd blended in.

Clarissa stood shivering in a thick gray down coat as she delivered the story for live news.

Gia had wanted to talk to her. Now was her chance.

While Murphy orchestrated the rescues and transportation as the church van arrived, Gia maneuvered her way over to the anchorwoman.

She waited until Clarissa wrapped up the initial segment, then approached her.

"Special Agent Franklin." Clarissa pushed the microphone toward Gia. "Tourists and residents of Tinley are stricken with panic over this serial killer. Several told me that's the reason they braved the hazardous conditions today."

Gia's chest tightened as the reporter gestured toward the carnage of the pile-up. "Is it true you have a suspect in jail?"

Gia had no idea how the woman had gleaned that information. She glanced at Murphy, but he was too busy helping an elderly man into the church van to notice Clarissa.

"We are questioning a person of interest, but at this point, no formal charges have been filed, and we are not certain he is the CK." That would frighten people more, but she refused to lie or offer a false sense of safety.

"The investigation is ongoing, and my sister is still missing. Again, we ask anyone with information about this unidentified man or any of the murders to please call the police."

"Can you reveal the name of the man in custody?"

"Not at this time." Gia paused, planning her statement. "But I do want to address the man who kidnapped my sister. If you're watching, I know you have two ornaments left. Eleven and twelve. I ask that you spare my sister and come after me instead." She lifted her chin, ignoring Clarissa's startled look. "I'm the one who challenged you. I'm the one who has been chasing you for the past three weeks." She pressed a hand over her chest. "I'm the one you want, the one who'll make you famous."

She actually managed a smile, one filled with challenge again. "So, call me. Talk to me. Tell me where to come and I'll be there."

5:00 P.M., DECEMBER 19, TINLEY

Murphy grimaced at the sight of the reporter confronting Gia. A bad feeling seized his gut. What the hell was Gia up to? He knew she was desperate, but how desperate?

Someone called his name though, and he turned back to handle the situation at hand. Some motorists were already suffering from hypothermia and shock. He, Gia and the first responders were at danger for that themselves. All the more reason to work quickly.

Finally, the church van and ambulances headed toward the hospital.

Clarissa Klondike and her cameraman approached him. "Sheriff, can you comment on the panic spreading through town or give the public any idea when they will feel safe again in Tinley?"

Murphy shot her a warning look. She knew good and damn well he couldn't. But he wanted to calm the residents of Tinley, so he adopted a neutral tone. "Residents and tourists, please heed the warnings about Holly and be diligent about safety precautions. Stay alert. Watch out for anything out of the ordinary or anyone acting suspiciously. This man targets females, although who knows what he may do if confronted. If you think you see him or cross his path, do not attempt to apprehend him. Call the police."

He ended the interview, anxious to get Gia out of the elements and to question Folsom again.

His phone buzzed. Hoping it was a lead, not fallout from

the fear raging through town, he checked the number. Golden Gardens, the assisted living facility where his mother lived.

His heart thundered as he connected. "It's Murphy. What's going on?"

"Mr. Malone, it's Teresa, your mother's nurse. I'm afraid she took a fall. We're transporting her to the hospital for x-rays to determine if she broke her hip."

Dammit, broken hips could be dangerous for someone as frail as his mother. Her RA had progressed to the point that she could barely walk without a cane.

"I wouldn't have called, but she's asking for you, and... she's having chest pains. It's possibly just a panic attack, but we want a cardiologist to examine her."

Murphy ran a hand over his face. "I'll be there ASAP."

He hung up and trudged through the snow to his vehicle. Gia was huddled inside with the heater running.

"I have to go to the hospital," he said as he maneuvered onto the road. "My mom fell and may have broken her hip. She's also having chest pains."

Gia gently touched his arm. "I'm sorry, Murph. I know how much your mother means to you."

A muscle ticked in his jaw. "She'll be all right. She's tough."

But fear gnawed at him. His mother was all the family he had. And Gia understood about losing a mother.

"She will be okay, but you have to be with her," Gia agreed softly. "Drop me at the jail and I'll see if Folsom is ready to talk while you go to her."

Murphy didn't want to leave Gia. But he would come back to her, for the case. For Carly. And Sari.

And to see if something else was going on between him and the woman he'd always loved.

But he had to check on his mother first.

5:10 P.M., DECEMBER 19, TINLEY

Ten minutes later, Gia studied Folsom before closing the distance to the cell. He was agitated, pacing, twitching and cursing.

When he saw her, he came to a halt and gripped the bars of the cell. "Are you ready to let me go?"

"No," Gia said. "Not until you come clean with us."

"I've told you I didn't kill all those women!" Folsom bellowed.

"Just tell me where my sister is."

His eyes narrowed, then his voice calmed. But his tone was nasty. "You're wasting your time here with me. If she dies, it's your fault."

Gia reached out and yanked him by the throat. "She'd better not die," she hissed. "If she does, I'll put you in the grave."

Her cell phone buzzed on her hip. For a moment, her breathing was so erratic the sound didn't register.

"Where is she?" she shouted.

His fingers curled around her hands as he tried to loosen her grip. "You've got the wrong man. And you're going to pay for it."

Her phone trilled again, finally hacking through the fog of furry consuming her. She shoved the man away, then stepped back and jerked her phone from her pocket.

Dragging in a cleansing breath, she strode into the hall and checked the number.

Carly's.

Hands trembling, she connected. "Carly?"

"Help me."

A sob lodged in Gia's throat. "Where are you, honey?"

"Tree...Christmas tree..."

"Christmas tree...which one? Where are you?"

But the line went dead in her hand, cutting off her sister's response.

CHAPTER TWENTY-FIVE

5:15 P.M., December 19, Tinley

HE GENTLY WIPED a tear from Carly's cheek.

She was so beautiful and so much sweeter than her sister. It was a shame to have to kill her.

But it was part of his plan. And she'd seen too much. Knew too much now.

While the blizzard raged on, she'd talked to him, wanted to know what made him tick. Had asked as if she genuinely cared.

That was just an act though.

She was just stalling. Trying to keep herself alive.

Still, he'd indulged her by telling her that he'd first seen her sister where he'd posed Page. That had been a lie though. He'd seen her a long time ago and wanted to get to know her then.

But she'd ignored him.

She wasn't ignoring him now.

Gia was a worthy opponent, he told Carly. She hated Christmas as much as he did.

On some level, he knew she understood him, too.

"You don't have to do this," Carly whispered. "My sister and I need to be together this holiday. We lost our mother…."

"Don't worry," he murmured. "You'll all be together this year."

A sob escaped her. "Not that way though. I want Gia to remember we're still a family. You don't know her. She'll help you."

Oh, he knew her very well. More than any of the others." A bitter laugh escaped him. "Your sister wants to lock me in a cell for the rest of my life." A suffocating feeling tightened his chest at the thought of being confined in a six-by-eight-foot space with nothing but steel bars surrounding him. Lying on a threadbare cot at night where men acted like animals.

And the food tasted like crap.

"Please," Carly begged. "Just let me and my sister help you."

"You are going to help me," he murmured. "You're going to help me finish out the Twelve Days of Christmas."

Then he pressed a kiss to her forehead and left her to wait.

CHAPTER TWENTY-SIX

6:10 P.M., December 19, Tinley

AT THE HOSPITAL, Murphy rushed to the nurses' desk and identified himself.

"Yes, Sheriff. They've taken your mother for an EKG and then to x-ray. Let me show you to the ER room."

He followed the nurse to Room Seven and pushed the curtain aside to see an empty room. He stepped inside, battling the fear pressing against his chest.

After his mother kicked his old man to the curb, it had just been the two of them. She had to be all right.

Five long minutes later, an orderly wheeled his mother in. Her graying hair spiraled around her pale face, making her look small and ghostlike.

But her eyes seemed sharp as a cat's, as if she was searching for him.

"I'm here, Mom." He clutched her hand as the orderly shifted the gurney into the tiny room. "How are you feeling?"

"Like a danged fool for falling." She huffed. "Sorry for

dragging you over here in this storm. I know you have more important things to do."

Emotions clogged Murphy's throat. He lifted her frail hand in his and pressed a kiss to it. "Mom, nothing is more important than you."

His mother had always been kind. Loving. Taken care of him when he was sick. Encouraged him to be a good man. To stand up for what was right.

"Don't be silly, son. It's time you find someone of your own." She gave him that motherly look she used when admonishing him.

"I'm fine, Mom. I just want you to be okay."

A doctor in a white coat appeared and introduced herself as Dr. Kim Young. Then she placed a gentle hand on his mother's shoulder and smiled down at her. "Mrs. Malone, I have good news and bad news. Which do you want first?"

"Just give it all to me," his mother said in her no-nonsense fashion.

"First of all, then, your heart is fine. The chest pains you were experiencing were caused from anxiety over the fall."

Murphy exhaled in relief. "That's good, Mom."

Dr. Young gave him a sympathetic smile. "However, the x-ray did reveal that you fractured your hip. That's going to require surgery, and then some physical therapy," Dr. Young waited a heartbeat for them to react.

His mother clenched the sheet to her. "All righty then, let's get the ball rolling."

"Are you sure she's up for surgery?" Murphy asked.

"Like I said, her heart is in good condition. We will, of course, monitor it while we repair the fracture."

Murphy pushed a wiry strand of gray hair from her fore-head, knowing she would make the final decision. "Mom?"

"I said let's do it," she said. "I intend to walk at my son's wedding, not roll around in a wheelchair like some old lady cripple."

He had no plans for a wedding. Although Gia's face flashed in his mind and that kiss taunted him.

Would she leave as soon as this case was solved? Could they possibly have a future together?

She pulled him closer and he leaned in to hear her. "Now, I'll do my part and get well, Murphy. You do yours and find you a good woman."

Murphy pressed a kiss to her cheek, and watched them wheel her from the room, his heart in his throat.

6:15 P.M., DECEMBER 19, TINLEY

Carly's words reverberated in Gia's head. Christmas tree... she'd wanted her to decorate it with her...

Or had she been trying to give her a message?

The fact that the call had come shortly after her interview with Clarissa could be coincidental. Or maybe it was intentional, just as the killer had planned the murders.

If Folsom was the killer, he hadn't orchestrated the call or seen that interview. Which meant he was probably innocent, at least of the Twelve Days of Christmas murders.

Unless he'd carried Carly back to their childhood home after they'd searched it. And Carly had somehow gotten hold of a phone...

She had to see if Carly was there.

She reached for her phone to call Murphy but saw his text.

Mom broke her hip and is going into surgery. I need to be here for a while. Let me know if a lead comes through.

Indecision warred in her mind. She wanted him with her

more than she'd ever imagined. But she couldn't take him away from his mother at the hospital.

Still, she needed transportation. She texted Murphy.

Hope surgery goes well. Folsom still refuses to talk. I'm going to my old house to rest. Borrow a vehicle?

He responded immediately. *Sure. My Jeep is in the parking lot. Keys in my desk drawer. Be safe.*

She snagged his keys, then bundled up to tackle the outdoors. The wind nearly knocked her over as she pushed through the cold and snow to the Jeep. It took a few attempts to start the engine, and another few minutes for the defroster to clear the windshield enough for her to see the street.

Driving was treacherous and slow, but at least there were no other cars on the road. The few miles seemed to take forever, but thankfully, the Jeep's four-wheel drive helped her manage the sludge and ice. She kept her eyes peeled for an ambush as she pulled up the driveway and parked.

No vehicles in sight. No signs of tire tracks or any other mode of transportation.

Securing her gun in her jacket pocket, she tugged her scarf and coat around her and braced herself for the wind as she climbed out and maneuvered the path to the front door. Before checking the lock, she pulled her gun and held it at the ready.

If the CK was inside with Carly, he could be waiting.

Gia jiggled the door, but it was still locked, just the way she'd left it. Using her key, she unlocked it, then eased open the door.

The wind whistled through the eaves in a mind-numbing roar. The ancient wood floor creaked as she entered and scanned the foyer. Senses honed, she moved through the house, searching each room and closet.

Everything appeared as it had been the last time she was here.

Carly was not inside.

Frustration mounted on top of despair, and she returned to the living room with the bare Christmas tree and sank down in front of it, hoping for answers.

But the box of family ornaments waiting to be hung on the tree mocked her.

She picked up a tiny silver frame that held a picture of she and Carly, one when they were around three and five in candy cane pajamas. Her mother's favorite.

She traced a finger over Carly's sweet little face and began to sob like a baby. And she couldn't help but wish she had Murphy's arms around her, to provide an oasis from the storm of sorrow choking her.

8:15 P.M., DECEMBER 19, TINLEY

Two hours later, Murphy paced the hospital waiting room, sucking down coffee as he tried to remain positive. His mother was tough, at least mentally.

She would make it.

She had to.

He listened to the weather report. The governor had declared a state of emergency. For the next twenty-four hours, everyone was asked to stay hunkered inside. First responders were ordered to stay off the roads as well.

His phone vibrated. Cody.

"Hey, man, I was about to call you. Please tell me you found Carly," Murphy said.

"I wish I could." Cody's voice sounded tired, strained. "We've searched all the cottages and that extra outbuilding being renovated. Nothing."

"Are all the guests accounted for?" Murphy asked.

"All except one. A no-show for Cottage Six. Owner of the cottages said the guy cancelled because he was stranded in Colorado."

Murphy tensed. "A single guy?"

"Yeah."

"You get his name and contact information?"

"I did. I'm on my way back to the office. I'll run him through the system when I get there."

"Let me know what you find." Murphy explained about Folsom being in the holding cell. "Oh, and I just heard the weather. You need to call off the search teams temporarily. It's too dangerous to have our people out now."

"I hate to do that." Emotions thickened Cody's words. "I want to find her, man. I should have told her how I felt."

"I know." Murphy heard regret in his deputy's voice. He didn't want to have that same kind of regret with Gia.

"We aren't giving up," Murphy said.

"No, no way," Cody agreed. "See you back at the station."

"I'll be back as soon as possible." He walked over and stared out the window at the sea of white.

They might not know where Carly was yet. But with Holly unleashing her fury, the killer couldn't be out in it either.

He just prayed Gia stayed home, and that she was safe. He couldn't lose his mother *or* Gia tonight.

8:30 P.M., DECEMBER 19, TINLEY

Gia splashed cold water on her face. Her eyes were swollen and puffy now, her cheeks flushed.

She had to pull herself together.

Think.

If Carly had been giving her a message, and she wasn't referring to home, then where?

She strode back and forth in front of the picture window, shivering as Holly pounded them.

Christmas tree...

Childhood memories assaulted her. She and her family traipsing through the tree farm to choose the perfect tree. Then they'd chop it down, stow in it the cab of her dad's pick-up truck. After he died when she was five, it was just she and Carly and their mother.

She glanced back at the tree, then the pictures on the mantle. An eight-by-ten of she and Carly having a snowfall fight at the Christmas tree farm. Moira and Leon Hanes ran the place and sold hand woven wreaths and garland. A life-size sleigh and statuesque reindeer sat to the right of the shed, a favorite photography spot for families. She and her sister had climbed in that sleigh every year and smiled at their mother.

The visit was always fun, except for the Hanes' creepy son. Homer had been in charge of handing out axes and saws to the customers.

She studied the photograph again. Gossip had spread that Mr. Hanes was a mean drunk and beat his son. His wife just left one day, leaving Homer with his daddy. Then one day the Department of Family and Children's Services had been called. The old man ran off and Homer was sent to foster care.

Another owner bought the property and had been running it ever since. They'd torn down the Hanes farmhouse and built a sprawling ranch a couple of miles away.

But the shed where the tools were stored remained.

Her pulse jumped. With the farm closed because of the weather, that shed would be the perfect place to hide out.

Adrenaline churning, she dragged on her coat, snow

boots, gloves and hat, then snagged her purse and the keys to Murphy's Jeep. Walking to the vehicle was a challenge. Her calf muscles ached with the effort to move against the force of the wind, and the chill burned her exposed cheeks, stinging as if blades of ice were stabbing her face.

She ducked into the vehicle, fired up the engine and rumbled down the drive. Twice, she almost ran off the road, but managed to right herself before sliding into a ditch. Finally, she spotted the shed in the distance.

The sleigh and reindeer still stood in the same place. She slowed, scanning the property as she approached. No movement, except for the trees swaying and bending.

She screeched to a stop, gripped her gun at the ready, wrapped her scarf around her face and headed toward the shed.

Just as she reached it, she heard a scream.

"Run, Gia, run!"

Carly.

CHAPTER TWENTY-SEVEN

9:00 P.M., December 19, Tinley

GIA REACHED for the door handle to the shed, but a shadow moved behind her.

Two strong hands grabbed her into a chokehold. She kicked back and bucked, then tried to elbow her assailant, but he pressed a rag over her mouth and dragged her through the snow.

Cold and ice bit at her through her clothing. The world spun. Darkness beckoned.

Carly! She tried to scream her sister's name, but the sound died in the violent wind gusts.

Think. Fight.

But a fog enveloped her brain, and the world slipped out of focus. She struggled to wrench free, but her limbs suddenly felt weighted. Lifeless. She couldn't move them.

Then she collapsed into the darkness.

10:15 P.M., DECEMBER 19, TINLEY

Night was setting in. The storm was intensifying.

Murphy hadn't heard from Gia in hours.

He called her for the dozenth time while he waited on his mother to wake up from surgery. She'd made it through the procedure and was in recovery.

No answer on Gia's phone.

Murphy pressed her number again. *Dammit, Gia, pick up.*

It rang and rang, but nothing. What in the hell? Where was she?

Were the cell towers down?

He punched Cody's number. "Have you heard from Special Agent Franklin?"

"No, was I supposed to?"

"No, but she's not answering her phone," Murphy said.

"Maybe it's not charged," Cody said. "Or she decided to sleep a while."

Gia's words taunted him. *I won't rest until I find Carly.*

"Are you at the jail?" Murphy asked.

"Yes."

"Is my Jeep there?"

"Not in the parking lot."

Murphy scrubbed a hand over his face. He hoped to hell she was sleeping. He was bone tired himself. Gia had to be. "Gia took it to her house. I'm going by there and see if I can find her. Let me know if she shows up."

Cody agreed, and Murphy went to talk to the nurse. "Can I see my mother now?"

She bit her bottom lip. "For just a minute. She's pretty heavily sedated."

"I don't care. I have to go, but I need to see her first."

She conceded, and he followed her to the recovery area.

His mother lay so still that for a moment, emotions choked him.

The nurse touched his elbow. "She's all right," she murmured. "Just coming out of anesthesia."

Murphy breathed out, then stepped over to the bed and cradled her frail hand in his. "Mom?"

She moaned softly, then her eyes flickered open. "Murph?"

"I'm here, Mom. You made it through surgery. They'll be moving you to a room soon."

She squeezed his hand although her grip was so weak he barely felt it.

"I have to go," he said. "That case..."

"I know," she murmured, her voice slurred from the drugs. "Don't forget what I said. You need a woman."

He chuckled and kissed her on the forehead. He was thinking about it. Trouble was, the only woman he wanted was Gia Franklin.

Cold fear knotted his belly as he left his mother and hurried outside.

The five-minute drive took over twenty minutes. Twenty minutes of terrifying scenarios bombarding him.

Gia had never made it home. She'd been accosted on the way. *The Christmas Killer* had her.

Bile rose in his throat. He had to find her, save her, tell her that he cared about her.

In spite of the freezing temperature, he was sweating by the time he finally reached the Franklin house. The driveway was empty. He parked, then climbed out and shined his flashlight on the path to the door in search of footprints or signs that she'd been there.

Twigs and debris littered the steps, and indentations in the snow indicated Gia—or someone else—had been here. The same on the porch.

He jiggled the door, and it opened easily.

A cold sense of dread ripped through him.

He pulled his gun and entered, scanning the entryway and beyond. The floor was damp, the wet stains about the size of a woman's boots.

"Gia!"

A hollow emptiness echoed back, followed by the raging wind beating at the farmhouse.

He hurried through the kitchen and into the living area where he spotted the Christmas tree waiting. The box of ornaments sat beside it. Several lay on the floor as if Gia had been looking through them.

No Twelve Days ornaments though.

No Gia either.

He searched the house. Empty.

A half full teacup sat on the kitchen counter, left unfinished. Beside the teacup, sat a framed photograph of Gia and her sister posing at the Christmas tree farm.

Murphy gripped the edge of the table with clammy hands.

Where the hell was she?

11:30 P.M., DECEMBER 19, TINLEY

Gia had no idea how long she'd been unconscious. She'd been in and out for a while though. But each time she woke, she was too weak to do anything.

Because this sicko had injected her with that paralytic drug. What was he waiting for? Why not just kill her?

Did he need the storm to lift so he could choose the perfect place to pose her and Carly with those damn Christmas ornaments?

Thoughts jumbled together, nausea rolling through her. Murphy's strong handsome face taunted her.

She hadn't wanted to take him away from his mother. She had to be independent.

But she could have called someone. Brantley. Murphy's deputy.

Why hadn't she?

She could have trusted Murphy. She did trust him. She admired him, too.

She always had. Had always wanted him. Maybe that was the reason she hadn't dated anyone seriously since. Murphy had stolen her heart years ago and she'd never gotten it back.

God help her, she wanted to tell him that. But her brain was fuzzy again. The drugs and nausea robbed her energy and sanity, and she gave into it and closed her eyes.

The next time she stirred, her hands and feet were bound, and a gag was stuffed in her mouth, nearly choking her. But she could move again. The drug was wearing off.

Still, it was so dark she couldn't see anything. And cold, as if she was locked in a space with no heat.

She raked her hand across the floor and touched wood, then a wall. More wood. Curved. Metal above her.

A building? The shed at the tree farm?

The scent of pine and fertilizer hit her. Then the smell of fear.

A second later, she heard breathing.

Heart pumping, she yanked at the gag with her bound hands and pulled it away. "Carly?"

A low moan, then the breathing sped up, more erratic.

"Carly, honey, it's Gia. Are you in here?"

A whimper, then a cry. Gia scooted across the floor. "Carly, I'm here. It's okay."

Gia reached out her hands and felt her sister's soft hair, then her face. She yanked the gag from Carly's mouth.

"It's okay, take deep breaths." She traced her hands over

Carly's hair, then her tear-dampened face, checking for injuries.

"Did he hurt you?" Gia asked through clenched teeth.

Carly grabbed her hands and clenched them. "I'm all right..." she said between gasps. "He...drugged me."

"I know," Gia said, hatred for the man rising from the depths of her soul. "I'm so sorry, sweetie."

"Not your f...ault," Carly murmured. "I'm j...ust glad you're here..."

Guilt washed over her. She should have come sooner. Then Carly might be safe.

"I've been scared out of my mind ever since you called," Gia said in a strangled voice.

She pulled her sister as close as she could, reassuring her with promises that they'd escape, then they'd trim the Christmas tree together.

Just as soon as she nailed this psycho.

There was no way in hell she'd let him finish the Twelve days, not by adding her and her sister to his body count.

12:10 A.M., DECEMBER 20, TINLEY

Murphy continued to call Gia's number, but each time it rolled straight to voice mail.

Something was wrong. He felt it in his gut.

Had she made contact with the killer? Had she figured out where he was holding her sister and gone after her on her own?

That would be so like Gia. Not to ask for help.

Dammit, he wanted to be there for her. Show her she wasn't completely alone. That he'd always be there for her.

Maybe she'd talked to her partner at the FBI.

He called the field office Gia was assigned to and explained the situation. "I'll have Special Agent Harmon contact you as soon as we hang up," the agent said.

He ended the call and sat down at the table with his head in his hands. The picture on the table mocked him. Carly and Gia, happy when they were little.

Christmas, the time of year when families and the town of Tinley celebrated life and home and family and love.

Yet this year Holly had destroyed the festivities, his mother was in the hospital, residents and tourists were panicked, a woman was missing, and another one dead in his town.

And now Gia was gone.

Find a good woman, Murphy.

He had. Now he just had to save her from that monster.

The sound of his phone trilling startled him, and he snatched it up.

"This is Special Agent Brantley Harmon. What happened to Gia?"

Murphy quickly relayed his concerns.

"I saw that interview she did with your local reporter," Brantley said. "For Pete's sake, she challenged the killer to come after her."

Murphy chewed the inside of his cheek. Gia wanted to save her sister, was willing to sacrifice herself. He didn't like it one damn bit. But he did understand it.

"I don't know where she is. I keep calling and no answer," Murphy gritted out, desperation building in his chest. "I'm at her sister's house and she's not here."

"Let me see if I can trace her phone," Brantley told him.

Murphy thanked him and waited while the man set the trace into motion. "Listen," Brantley said. "Earlier, Gia asked me to pull footage of all the crime scenes and press conferences."

Murphy rubbed a hand across his forehead. "Yeah?"

"I may have something." Brantley cleared his throat. "There's a man who showed up at more than one crime scene, and he appears at the press conferences."

Often perpetrators hung around the crime scenes to watch the chaos and fear caused by their actions. "A reporter?"

"That's what I thought at first, and the reason he didn't draw suspicion. He had press credentials," Brantley said.

"But something's off about him?"

"The editor at the small press where he claimed he worked never heard of him."

Murphy released an expletive. "So, who is he?"

"His press ID read Leon Miller, but that's fake. I'm working on his real identity now. I'm also sending you his photograph."

The text dinged, and Murphy looked at the image. The man had short clipped dark hair. Was clean-shaven. Well dressed.

And...something about him looked eerily familiar. Had he seen the man in town?

CHAPTER TWENTY-EIGHT

12:15 A.M., December 20, Tinley

GIA AND CARLY CLUNG to each other for a moment. Gia's heart was hammering with worry. "I saw the blood on the floor in the shop. What happened, Carly? Where are you hurt?"

Carly squeezed Gia's hands. "It's nothing, sis. I just cut my hand when I reached out to snatch at the tree to stay on my feet."

"Did he say anything before he took you?" Gia asked.

"No, he just came into the store like he was looking for a gift. I told him I was about to close, that he could come back, then he grabbed me."

"Did you recognize him?"

Carly's breathing was finally starting to steady. "No... although something about him seems familiar. Maybe he's been to the festival before and shopped at my place last year."

Gia's breath tightened. "I'm so sorry, honey."

"He's sick," Carly said. "I faded in and out, but he kept

213

talking to me. Saying things about Christmas and how he hated it. How he'd bought these extravagant gifts for his wife, but she left him just like his mother did."

"Did he talk about the ornaments?"

"He said his mother used to celebrate the Twelve Days of Christmas by giving him a gift each day."

"That's the reason he chose the Twelve Days theme." Gia pulled her sister's hands toward her. "I'll untie you, then you can untie me."

Together they began to work at the rope knots. A sliver of light seeping in through the crack in the door allowed Gia to see Carly. Her fingers felt raw, cold, numb, but finally she managed to unravel the knot. "What about Parker Whitman? At first we thought he'd abducted you."

"No." Carly shook her head. "Parker's nice. We had coffee, but he was so hung up on his wife, that I encouraged him to work it out with her. He was flying home and going to suggest they attend marriage counseling."

So, Whitman had been innocent.

"Do you know a man named Folsom?"

"No, should I?"

"We have him in lock up. I thought he might be the CK. But he can't be as he's still in jail."

Carly's hands sprang free, and she began to work at Gia's ropes.

"But I wonder how he knew about this place," Gia said, thinking out loud.

"Maybe his family used to come here," Carly suggested as she loosened the ropes on Gia's wrists.

When Gia was free, she worked at the ropes around her ankles while Carly did the same.

The wheels of time and memory spun in Gia's head. She threw aside the ropes. "Carly, you said he sounded familiar.

Do you remember when we were little and used to come out here with Mom?"

"Of course, I do," Carly murmured.

"Remember that creepy boy Homer who used to give out the axes."

"Oh, my goodness, yes. You and I were just talking about him. He used to hide out in the woods with a saw and scare us when we were tree hunting."

"There were rumors that his father abused him, and his mother abandoned him." Her blood ran cold. "The profile fits."

"What are you saying?"

"That Homer Hanes might be the Christmas Killer."

12:20 A.M., DECEMBER 20, TINLEY

Murphy paced while Gia's partner ran the fake journalist's picture through facial recognition software.

His skin prickled with the sensation that Gia had left that photo of she and Carly on the table as a message.

"Hey, I got a hit," Brantley said. "Hanes. He's actually from—"

"Tinley," Murphy breathed, the truth dawning. "His parents owned the Christmas tree farm. Father's name was Leon." He pulled his keys from his pocket and ran for the door. "I think I know where he's holding Carly and Gia."

The agent was still on the phone as Murphy started the engine. "Hanes has a juvie record," Agent Harmon told him. "A foster parent reported him for abusing animals. Fast-forward to college and a girl filed charges of assault. Dropped them though and moved away. No word of what happened to her."

Murphy had a bad feeling. Perhaps she'd been his first kill. "See if you can find more on her. He could have murdered her and hidden the body."

Murphy battled the treacherous road as he drove toward the tree farm. "What happened to the mother?"

"I don't know, but I'm on it."

"Talk to his wife. Find out what she knows about him. Maybe she filed for divorce because she suspected he was a psycho."

He was half a mile from the farm when a tree snapped and splintered down in front of him. Murphy swerved to avoid hitting it but skidded off the side of the road. His SUV spun in a circle and careened sideways then stopped.

He shifted into gear and attempted to back up, but his tires spun, digging deeper and deeper into the ground and slinging snow and ice. He pounded the steering wheel with his fist. The road was blocked.

Wind snapped more branches and flung snow in a blinding haze. He had to keep moving though. Get to Carly and Gia.

He yanked on his snow cap and wrapped a scarf around his neck and face, then climbed from the vehicle.

The half-mile trek strained his calf muscles, and battered his body, but he kept moving. As he neared the tree farm, he scanned the property, but the whiteout conditions made it nearly impossible to see three feet in front of him.

Finally, as he drew closer, he spotted the shed. He pulled his gun, then moved toward it, braced for an attack.

12:45 A.M., DECEMBER 20, TINLEY

Gia tensed at the sudden sound. Not just the wind whistling.

Him.

Singing. "*The Twelve Days of Christmas.*"

Carly's eyes flashed with terror. "He's coming back."

Gia pressed her fingers over Carly's lips. "Shh. Stay calm. I'll protect you." She frantically began sweeping the floor and walls with her hands for a weapon. An ax. Shovel. *Anything.*

But the shed was empty.

Because he'd planned this.

Noise again. Homer's footsteps.

She patted her clothing for her phone or weapon, but the CK had confiscated them both. Desperate, she removed her boot and held it up, ready to attack.

Carly pressed her back against the wall, struggling with the ropes.

"Be still and curl up on your side away from him," Gia murmured. "Pretend you're still drugged."

Carly whimpered, but she did as Gia instructed. It pained Gia to see her sister look like a victim. But she had to think now. Set her own trap.

Not succumb to fear.

Darkness engulfed the interior space, sucking the air and light. It was so cold that Gia's hands were beginning to feel numb.

She gripped the boot in her hand and angled her arm, preparing an attack. The shed door screeched open, a faint sliver of light from the man's pin light shining across the dank interior.

Carly was shivering from the cold, unable to keep her cries silent. He seemed drawn to her anguish as he shuffled toward her.

"Shh, it'll be over soon, Carly." Then he angled the light

away from her sister toward the opposite wall where he'd left Gia.

~~She lunged at him like a banshee and swung the boot at~~ his head. She connected, hitting him in the side of the face and sending him reeling against the wall.

He bellowed, momentarily shaken and stunned, then shoved away from the wall and lunged toward her. She balled her hand into a fist, but before she could deliver a blow, he swung a shovel toward her.

She ducked but not in time. The hard metal connected with her temple and sent her down. Stars swam in front of her eyes, and the world spun.

Carly jumped up and threw herself on the man's back. He hurled her off, and she hit the side of the shed with a whack. Gia struggled to push herself up, but the cold barrel of her own gun stabbed her cheek and she froze, afraid to move.

Afraid he'd kill her before she could get her sister out of this mess.

She had to stall. Keep him talking.

"Why here, Homer? Why at your childhood home?"

His breath hissed out. He smelled of cigarettes and sweat, a sign he wasn't as cool as he pretended. "Because I hated it here. Daddy made me clean up after everyone, chop up all the dead trees. Every day I watched all these smiling, screaming kids run around the woods, pointing out which tree they wanted. Then the family would pose for pictures in that damn sleigh. Happy families. Sickening."

Gia's mind raced. "Sickening because your family wasn't happy?"

"When I was little, I thought they were. Then Daddy started drinking and was mean. He acted so nice to all the customers, but when everyone left, he turned into a monster."

A picture of Homer hiding behind the trees and frightening her and her sister flashed through her mind. He'd looked like a wild animal sometimes. Had he been acting out aggressions because he was a victim of childhood abuse? "He hurt you, abused you," she said. "Did you tell anyone?"

He shoved her against the wall, the cold metal of the gun brushing her skin. Carly lay still on the floor, unconscious from the blow. Gia fought through her rage. Getting Homer to talk would work in her favor.

Maybe she could even convince him to relinquish the weapon.

"Mama knew," Homer said. "She tried to stop him, but he turned on her."

"Did she call the police? Reach out for help?"

"No, she just walked out one day, disappeared, and left me here with him."

Had she walked out and left him? Or...had Homer's father done something to her? He could have killed her and buried her anywhere on this tree farm.

Gia made a mental note to have police search for a body once she and Carly were safe.

"I'm sorry that happened to you," Gia said. "Really sorry, Homer. Carly and I would have been your friends if we'd known."

He made a sarcastic sound, his gun hand trembling. "No, you wouldn't. You were the goody-goody girls. You were scared of me."

She realized part of him had enjoyed instilling that fear in them. He'd gotten his first taste of the adrenaline rush from terrifying someone smaller than him.

"What about your wife? She must have loved you to marry you."

His bitter look pierced her. "She said she did. Then she up and left, too. I had presents for her. Twelve of them, one for each day, but she said she didn't want gifts from me. She didn't want anything except to be free."

Gia twisted her hands together. "What happened to her, Homer? Did she leave or did you hurt her?"

"She said she didn't want presents, but I gave her one anyway."

"What did you give her?"

"I let her live." His bitter chuckle rattled in the air as he yanked a red scarf from inside his jacket.

She summoned her strength to fight him, but he raised the gun and slammed it against her head. Pain ricocheted through her temple as she fell into nothingness.

Then she felt his hands sliding the scarf around her throat.

CHAPTER TWENTY-NINE

1:00 A.M. DECEMBER 20, Tinley

HE HAD it all planned out. The two little girls who'd whispered and run from him when he was a boy were all his now.

This Christmas was going to be the best ever!

He stooped down and ran his fingers over Gia's thick dark hair. It felt surprisingly soft, unexpectedly so with her cutthroat personality.

Unconscious, with her hand curled beneath her head and her lips slightly parted, she almost looked like a nice girl.

But she chased killers because she had a dark side herself. That was the only way she could do it.

She liked the hunt.

The hunt was over.

He checked his watch. It was almost Christmas. Outside Holly raged on, cocooning them into their own private world.

A world he'd once hated. Now it seemed fitting to be back here. Back where it all began. Back to the town that had been blind to what was really happening on the farm, where they came to smile and take their happy family pictures.

Back to the two girls he'd wanted to like him.

Now it didn't matter. He'd learned how fickle women were. His mother. That girl in college. The wife who'd promised to love, honor and cherish him, then cheated on him.

Gia moaned and lifted her fingers as if clawing for a way to push herself up.

"It's too late," he crooned. "I have to finish."

But he wanted them both awake when he strangled them.

Then he'd pose them in the sleigh for their yearly family holiday picture. They would be waiting, holding their ornaments, when the sheriff came looking for them.

And *he* would be long gone. Back to his life for another year. To eleven months of bliss until the nightmare of the holiday descended again.

CHAPTER THIRTY

MURPHY CURSED Holly as he stumbled through the snowy, frostbitten haze. Ahead he spotted his Jeep.

He was right. Gia was here.

No other vehicles. Only an ATV parked near the shed. That must be how the killer had been maneuvering during the storm.

Gripping his gun, he ignored the biting sting of the wind and climbed the small hill toward the shed. Just as he reached the crest, he noticed movement.

A shadow. No, a man. He was walking toward the sleigh, carrying something in his arms.

Not just something. A body.

Carly? Gia?

Please, dear God, don't let them be dead.

Adrenaline surged through him, and he crouched low and moved to the right to weave between the trees on the edge of the farm. The man was struggling to remain standing as he

223

carried the woman to the sleigh. A red scarf dangled from his pocket.

Murphy ran toward him, pushing through the foggy blizzard. Just as he neared him, another movement caught his eye.

Gia raced from the shed, fighting the wind to reach the man.

She screamed something, but the sound died in the wind. Then she started pummeling the man from behind.

He shoved Gia, and she stumbled backward and fell from the sleigh, arms and hands flailing for balance. Murphy hurried toward them and raised his gun.

"It's over, Hanes. Don't move or I'll shoot."

The only part of the man that was visible was his eyes, which looked crazed, shocked that he'd been caught.

A laugh echoed in the air as he lunged toward Gia.

Murphy fired once, then twice, nailing the guy in the chest. Hanes' body bounced backward, blood spraying the snow.

Gia screamed, jumped up and climbed the sleigh to her sister. Murphy kept his gun on Hanes and inched forward, then knelt and searched for a weapon. He found Gia's gun in the guy's pocket, removed it and shoved it inside his jacket. Then he checked for a pulse.

Hanes was breathing. Alive.

Good. Death was too easy for this twisted killer.

He should be forced to face the families of his victims.

Leaving the man bleeding and unconscious on the ground, he jumped onto the sleigh. Gia was leaning over her sister, sobbing her name. The red scarf around Carly's neck fluttered around her face in the wind. The Eleven Lords-A-Leaping ornament dangled from her wrist.

Was Carly his final victim?

1:25 A.M., DECEMBER 20, TINLEY

Fear pulsed through Gia, squeezing the air from her lungs. "Come on, Carly, you have to be okay. I can't lose you." She unwound that damn scarf, gasping at the sight of the ligature marks around her baby sister's throat.

Please, God, no...she couldn't have lost Carly. She was the only family Gia had left. She had so much to make up to her.

"Please, sis, open your eyes," Gia pleaded.

Murphy eased up beside her, lifted Carly's arm and checked for a pulse. Her gaze met his, panic pounding in her chest.

Time stood still. Wind beat at them. Snow covered their hoods and clothing. Trees snapped and broke.

She squeezed her sister's hands in hers. "Come on, sweetie, we have a tree to decorate. I can't do it without you." Her voice cracked, the tears flowing, and she laid her head against Carly, clinging to her.

A second later, Murphy touched her shoulder. "She has a pulse, Gia."

His words barely registered, but when they did, she lifted her head and looked up at him through her tears.

"She's alive," he said. "But we need to get her to the hospital."

Relief gushed through Gia. "You saved her. You saved *us*," Gia cried.

He gave her a quick kiss on the lips, hot and tender and full of promises, then he scooped Carly in his arms and carried her down from the sleigh then over to the Jeep. Shaking, Gia ran ahead and opened the door to the back seat, then tossed him the keys when he got to the car so he could heat up the engine.

He placed Carly in the front seat, and she wrapped a blanket around her sister.

Together, they dragged Hanes toward the Jeep and hauled him into the back seat. She handcuffed him then crawled in beside him.

Murphy slid into the driver's seat and headed toward the hospital. Everywhere Gia looked the countryside was bathed in darkness and white. Power lines were out and trees were swaying, battered now by the intensity of the storm.

Holly unleashed her worst just as they arrived and hurried inside with Carly and Hanes. Thankfully the hospital had back-up generators, so it still had power. Murphy accompanied Hanes as the medics wheeled him to the ER and stood guard over him while he was prepped for surgery.

Gia stayed with her sister to be examined, although the first thing she did was to cut that damn ornament off of her sister's wrist and bag it for evidence to use against Hanes.

He would spend the rest of his Christmases in prison.

She would spend hers with Carly.

CHAPTER THIRTY-ONE

Noon, December 24, Tinley

"White Christmas" played in the background as Gia and Carly hung the last of the decorations on the balsam fir, then stepped back to admire the twinkling lights and shining star on top.

The handmade ones from their childhood were special. So were the memories they'd made as a family.

But Gia wanted new memories. She and Carly had agreed to celebrate the holiday together in their mother's honor. While they still mourned their mother, they rejoiced in the fact that they'd both survived a crazed serial killer.

Hanes had survived surgery and was still in the hospital, although he would be transported to a prison hospital as soon as the roads cleared. When the snow melted, teams would search the tree farm for Mrs. Hanes' body. According to Brantley, she'd just disappeared. No trace of her after she'd supposedly abandoned her son.

Folsom had been released, too. Apparently, neighbors

confirmed that his wife had cheated on him, then falsely accused him of abusing her. Whether there would be fallout from Folsom, as he'd promised, she didn't yet know. And right now, it didn't matter. She just cared about Carly.

Murphy discovered that a group of teenage boys had stumbled on the bloody deer Folsom had dragged to the woods. They'd stuffed it in the refrigerator at the abandoned house as a prank.

Holly had raged through so quickly the town had been paralyzed for a day, but the storm had moved on now.

Road crews had worked diligently on major highways, and crews had already cleared local streets. The town had decided to salvage what they could of the holiday activities. The residents of Tinley had proven their resilience and were determined to make visitors feel welcome and give them hope.

Today featured a special Christmas tree lighting, along with carolers, followed by holiday cookie decorating and crafts in the town hall. Stores had opened up for last minute gift shopping with Santa Claus visits up until noon. After that, Santa would visit the hospital to hand presents out to the children. The church also had organized a special holiday meal and festivities at Golden Gardens. And a prayer service had been held for Sari, one of Hanes' victims.

Gia and Carly had chosen to stay tucked in their family home today. The scent of turkey and dressing and homemade apple pie wafted through the old farmhouse. Gingerbread and sugar cookies sat on plates alongside peppermint sticks and a pitcher of eggnog. The wine was chilling in the frig.

The doorbell dinged, and Carly started to get up from the rocker by the fire. "Stay put, sis, I'll get it."

"I'm not an invalid," Carly protested.

"I know, but you've been through a lot." Tears stung Gia's eyes as she gave her sister a hug, then she rushed to answer the door.

Cody arrived first with roses for her sister, proving Murphy's theory about his deputy having a crush on Carly true. Almost losing her had made him realize he'd needed to come clean with his feelings. He'd stayed at the hospital around the clock until Carly had been released. Gia definitely envisioned a future for those two with marriage and babies, the family her sister wanted and deserved.

As for herself...

Another engine burst into the sound of ice cracking off the trees outside, and Murphy climbed from his Jeep. He walked around to the passenger side, lifted his mother from the front seat and helped her up to the porch.

Gia welcomed them both and ushered him inside where he helped his mother onto the sofa. She'd come through surgery and was healing at Golden Gardens, but Gia insisted he bring her over for Christmas Eve dinner.

"Families should be together for Christmas," she told Murphy. "No one should be alone." She'd remembered the last few years when she'd chosen that for herself.

Never again.

Murphy gave her a kiss on the cheek. "Thanks."

She smiled up at him. "Thanks for coming."

They walked over to the buffet in the dining room, and she poured a shot of whiskey and herself a glass of wine.

His dark gaze met hers, probing. Serious. "When are you going back to Florida?"

Gia's heart stuttered at the thought of leaving. It had been her plan all along when she'd first come here. Save her sister, catch a killer, then move on to another case. Just another day on the job.

But now everything had changed. She wanted a life. To be near Carly.

To have a family of her own.

She smiled up at Murphy, amazed she'd been so stupid to think he was small town. "I'm considering a transfer."

His thick dark brow rose. "A transfer? Where to?"

She shrugged, her heart melting at the hope that flickered in his eyes. "The field office closest to here."

A smile tilted the corners of his sexy mouth. "I know someone who would like that."

"Carly?"

He chuckled and pulled her to him. "No, I would." He twisted her hair between his fingers. "I would like that very much."

She laughed, a soft, flirty sound that seemed foreign to her. But it felt right. Then she did what she'd wanted to do ever since he'd rescued she and Carly.

She pressed her lips to his and kissed him with all the love she had in her heart.

TINLEY 7 NEWS

"Happy Holidays, folks! This is Meteorologist Bailey Huggins coming to you live from Channel 7 Tinley News."

Bailey stood, hunched in her winter coat, in front of the "Welcome to Tinley" sign, just as she had a few days ago to warn residents and tourists about the approaching storm of the century.

Except today her broadcast carried a more optimistic tone.

"It's Christmas Eve, and I'm happy to report that Holly, the blizzard known as the bomb cyclone, that created havoc for tourists and residents the last few days, has left us.

"While Nebraska suffered massive property damage and a devastating loss of cattle and crops, the people of our great state are resilient and will recover. The temperature has risen to a whopping thirty-five degrees this afternoon. And with the sun battling its way through the winter storm clouds, the temperature is expected to rise to forty by nightfall, with wind gusts dying down to five to ten miles per hour. That means the sub-zero wind chill factor is no longer a problem.

All this, just in time for Santa to load his sleigh with presents and begin his trek across the world tonight!"

She gestured to the foot-deep snowdrifts piled on each side of the road. "Already local residents have been digging out and are determined to carry on the Christmas Festival that put the town on the map. Snowplows have been working all day to clear roads, stores have opened for last minute shopping, and a special service features caroling and the lighting of the twenty-foot Christmas tree in the heart of the town.

She hesitated. "As we say goodbye to Holly, we pray for those folks in our neighboring states as they bear the brunt of what we have just lived through."

She signed off, then walked over to the news van and climbed inside. She and her crew planned to celebrate the power of the human spirit and the end of Holly as Tinley residents joined for a special Christmas Eve service.*

Thanks for reading! If you enjoyed this book, please do leave a review.

Read on for a sneak peek of the next STORM WATCH novel, *Black Ice* by Regan Black.

SNEAK PEEK

BLACK ICE
STORMWATCH, Book 4
by Regan Black

"Good evening. I'm Joyce Adams for Channel Five Weather. The National Weather Service has just released an updated warning for our area for winter storm Holly. The outlook here in Deadwood is not improving.

...ter inundating Nebraska with record accumulations, ...olly is determined to keep snow plows and salt trucks in business here in South Dakota. Previous predictions that we should expect two to four feet of snow have been increased to six to eight feet in some areas. Drifts to ten or twelve feet are possible, with the high winds associated with Holly.

"If those numbers sound impossible, that's because we haven't seen a storm like this in eighty years. Now is the time to check your emergency supplies. You can find a list at our website, or use the ticker at the bottom of your screen. Please, double check your emergency plans and be prepared for road closures as early as tomorrow morning.

"Trooper Bob, our correspondent from the South Dakota Highway Patrol, has more information. Over to you, Trooper Bob."

Chapter 1

Deadwood, South Dakota

With her laptop perched on her knees and ear buds in her ears, Evelyn Cotton hit refresh, hoping this time the man she was scheduled to chat with would be in the online meeting room. Thanks to technology, it was her first face-to-face meeting with a potential investor in the family business she was trying to save.

Except he wasn't showing up and she couldn't sit here staring at the screen forever. She had to get over to the casino for her evening shift. This time of year, wild winter storms or not, dealing poker at the Silver Aces kept this family in the black.

Barely.

The investor, Tate Cordell, had contacted Cottonwood Adventures a few weeks ago. They'd hit it off over the phone and he'd requested a personal tour to get a feel for the area and a better idea of her plans to expand and offer winter activities. She was happy to oblige, but he'd cancelled last week's visit at the last moment, after she'd traded away her shift. With the sudden weather system jacking up flights and travel plans, they'd opted for an online meeting.

"Come on, Tate."

"He called?" her father, Dale, half-shouted from his beloved recliner. He'd spent the day in his woodshop, restoring a set of kitchen chairs for a friend.

"No." She shook her head. "Must be trouble with the connection."

"Or he lost interest."

Gee thanks. Evelyn suppressed a scathing glare. It was bad enough sitting here as if she'd been stood up by a date. "He'll call." She reached for her boots and pulled them on. When he *did* show—and he *would*—she wanted to make the most of every remaining minute.

"Then what's with the boots?"

She forcibly reminded herself that her dad loved her, even when he didn't show it in normal ways or even in ways she might prefer. Plus, big storms like the one closing in on them usually amped up his depression issues. "There's no sense wrecking my good shoes crossing the parking lot," she replied. If the meeting with Tate went well, this might be her last winter at the casino. Her heart actually fluttered at the happy thought.

For several seasons now, her father had posed significant resistance to her many suggestions and ideas that would shift Cottonwood from merely scraping by as an average three-season tour operation to a thriving year-round profitable endeavor. Whether or not he believed she could do it, he seemed determined to prevent her from trying. None of her spreadsheets or marketing plans had changed his mind. All she needed to put them on the map was a modest financial investment for new gear, a storage building, a website over-haul and a couple of new hires. *All* sounded like a lot, but she knew how to prioritize and make every penny stretch.

Her father, despite the evidence in the roof over his head and food on the table, wasn't convinced of her ability. Every time she asked, Dale refused to even consider a business loan, leaving Evelyn to get creative.

"I wish you'd stay home." He pointed at the television, where another aspiring journalist was bundled up against the gusting wind and blowing snow. "It's going to get worse in a hurry."

"It's a wonder the mic doesn't freeze over," she muttered. Her laptop chimed and she scrambled back in front of the camera, only to see that the meeting had timed out without starting. The chime was an email alert from the casino. Small comfort to know the internet connection was fine on her end. "Damn."

Her father snorted, either agreeing with her assessment or disapproving of her vocabulary. It didn't matter. She and Dale hadn't seen eye to eye on much of anything since her mother, Tess, died during Evelyn's senior year of college.

"Only goes to show you shouldn't be out in this mess," he said.

"I wish it was as easy as calling in," she said. "My boss just asked me to confirm I can make tonight's shift and she's hoping I'll stick around to work through the storm."

"You told me they were evacuating the resorts."

"Dad." Evelyn clung to her last scrap of patience as she turned off her laptop and stowed it away. Tate would resched-ule. It helped to remember that he wasn't the only backup plan she had working. "They were discussing the option. If people can't get out of town, they'll need entertainment." She'd packed an overnight bag and stowed it in her car, just in case the roads were impassable and she had to stay over.

"You're risking your neck just so they won't miss a dollar," he grumbled when she crossed the room to tell him goodbye.

She could launch into a lecture about the economic boost the casinos brought to Deadwood with events and tourism every single month. The Silver Aces even recommended Cottonwood Adventures to guests when the company was open. She could mention how the casinos reinvested a generous chunk of their profits back to the community year after year. She could, but she'd be wasting her breath.

"There's meatloaf in the fridge when you're ready." She wrapped her scarf around her neck and kissed her dad's graying hair before shrugging into her coat. Grabbing her overnight bag, she escaped her well-meaning father and headed for her car.

Between the wind and the temperature drop, the air had more bite as she stepped outside. She leaned into the wind, averting her face and wishing she'd parked in the garage. Thankfully, her compact SUV started right up with the same dependability it had shown for years. She turned on her radio for some upbeat music to perk up for her shift. Tate being a no show was a bummer, but dwelling on that disappointment would negatively impact her tips. Unfortunately, her favorite station was in full storm-mode.

"People." Winter Storm Holly was becoming a local obsession. She navigated the winding driveway from her life-long home, past the turn off for the Cottonwood Adventures office and to the main road. "It's not our first brush with snow." She laughed at herself, eyeing the remains of the most recent snowfall lining the shoulders on either side of the road and covering the wilderness in a blanket of white.

Traffic was lighter than she expected and, once she was

out of the driveway, the roads were mostly clear. Though she'd lived here all her life, it was hard even for her to imagine six feet of snow at the minimum. Maybe people were being smart and heeding the warnings to prepare for the worst. While that was the smart and safe way to go, it could cost her on a night when she needed the tips.

She was almost to the casino before she found a station still playing pop remakes of Christmas classics. It was enough to put a smile on her face as she finished the drive and circled for the closest parking space she could find.

As she gathered her purse and the bag with her good shoes, her cell phone rang. "Come on, Dad," she groaned. But she brightened when the screen showed Tate Cordell's number. Sucking in a quick breath, she pulled off her glove and swiped the screen to answer. "Cottonwood Adventures, Evelyn speaking."

"Evelyn!" He sounded slightly out of breath. "I am so, so sorry I didn't make our appointment."

She stopped herself before she spewed platitudes and nonsense that he shouldn't worry about it. It was time to change tactics. She'd been far too accessible in their prior conversations. He was a busy man, but she was no slouch.

"I hope everything is well," she said neutrally. "I'm about to head into another meeting." It wasn't a lie, she'd be meeting plenty of people on her shift. And she did need to speak with the manager on the hospitality side of the casino operations about her recent proposal for team-building excursions and events. "Please, send me an email and we can reschedule. Have a great—"

"Hang on." His tone hardened. "My internet connection went out."

"I hate it when that happens," she sympathized. The weather was already draining the warm air from the car. Her ungloved hand was getting chilled. "Whenever it's back up and running, send that email."

"You promised me a tour of the area."

Her cold fingers were quickly forgotten. He still planned to visit? He'd agreed to her outrageous price of a thousand dollars for a glorified walk through the woods, despite it being a snow-heavy season. They'd scheduled for the day after tomorrow and she'd assumed, especially after he didn't make the online meeting that he'd intended to delay the entire thing. "You're in Deadwood?"

"Almost," he replied. "Travel is interesting at best, but yes, I changed my plans to get ahead of the storm."

"Holly is a beast," she agreed as a gust sent snow swirling across her windshield. "And I'm afraid the last update said the storm was barreling straight for us. We really should postpone until the worst has passed."

"If I can get in tonight?"

His tenacity, the press in his voice, surprised her. "I'm not available until tomorrow at the earliest." Maybe not then if she had to cover for a coworker.

"What do you recommend?"

"With this storm?" She looked up at the heavy gray sky, gloomier still as evening deepened and the light faded. "I recommend you wait it out. The wilderness will still be here once Holly blows over and everyone can dig out."

"Dig out?"

She hadn't asked, but she got the impression Tate had been raised in a warm climate. "They're predicting several feet of snow accumulation. Factor in the drifts and it could be difficult if not impossible to get around for a few days."

"I didn't realize."

Loosely translated into business-speak, that meant she wouldn't be getting an influx of cash anytime soon. Worse, she might have just botched the deal, giving him the impression this was winter every year. She scrambled to salvage something from the call. "A winter storm like this one isn't something we see often, not even up here. As I explained earlier, the winter activities we want to offer won't be interrupted by inclement weather any more often than we experience in other seasons."

"I understand, Evelyn."

Oh, she hoped he did. More importantly, she needed him to trust her lifelong expertise in the area and her innovative expansion plans. Tate Cordell had surprised her when he'd reached out, but to date his continued interest in Cottonwood remained the most promising solution to propel the family business into profitable and sustainable territory for the long term.

There was a rapid tapping noise on his end before he spoke again. "I'll keep an eye on the weather and be in touch."

The call ended before she could say thank you.

Chilled again, she shoved her cell phone into her purse and put her glove back on for the dash across the parking lot.

Stan, a friendly face from high school, was the security guard on duty at the employee entrance. He held the door open for her as she rushed toward the building. "Evening," he said. "I hope you did all your storm prep before coming in."

She smothered the scream building in her throat. "Sure did," she replied. It wasn't Stan's fault that no one knew how to have a conversation about anything other than snowstorms right now. "Dad is all prepped at home and I have an overnight bag packed in the car, just in case I need to stay on and cover shifts."

"You really are set," he said with a smile. "Have a good shift, Evelyn."

She returned the sentiment as she walked away. Back here behind the scenes, the casino had designed a pleasant-enough area, though the focus was on utility rather than creating the posh experience everyone maintained out front for guests.

Stowing her coat and scarf in a locker, along with her boots, she slipped into the heels that completed the uniform and prepared for her shift. There weren't any new notices regarding players or problems, so when it was time, she strolled out to the casino.

It was her habit to take a circuit of the casino floor before taking her place at a table in the poker room. The routine helped her get a feel for the general vibe in and around the casino. Sometimes social events, big parties, or business groups amped up the energy and made everyone feel lucky. She had a similar habit when she guided tours with Cotton-wood Adventures, always spending a few minutes by herself taking in the weather before loading gear or heading out.

Tonight, the guests seemed upbeat overall. She didn't hear any chatter about the weather, not even around the slot machines. There were the usual grumbles about luck, but the staff worked together to make sure no one turned mean or disruptive. Although the casino wasn't at full capacity, business was brisk, which was a good sign for her potential tips.

Evelyn opened her table for Texas Hold'em and the poker room host filled it immediately with four men she guessed were traveling together for business judging by the button-down shirts open at the collar and the khaki slacks that had probably been freshly creased this morning. The loafers were the big clue. No local in his right mind wore loafers in Dead-wood at this time of year.

She found the group amusing with their friendly banter and superb poker-table manners. The various strategies they each attempted to convince the others to fold were hysterical. They played for an hour straight before one man excused himself to take a phone call from his wife.

Between hands, they discussed local attractions and

dinner options. She dutifully recommended a casino restaurant without bringing up the adverse weather conditions. It would've been nice to suggest a winter walk or a sledding adventure, but Cottonwood didn't have those options yet. Not for the public anyway.

Other players came and went as seats opened up. The current game was tight as a drum and conversation declined as the betting increased. The intensity was palpable, though it was Evelyn's job to keep up the impression that every player in the game had an equal chance.

She relaxed a bit more as the hours ticked by and the players changed. Sure, she preferred working outside in tennis shoes or hiking boots instead of heels, but on days like today, the casino had become her salvation.

In here, with no clocks, she could pretend she wasn't running out of time for the business or for her personal goals. Her only task was to perpetuate the illusion that a life-changing jackpot was almost within reach. Beyond the tips, a shift at the casino also gave her a marvelous break from the constant news and weather warnings for the area. A customer might mention it in passing, but then someone would change the bet, or grimace, and the focus would shift back to the game.

There could be one snowflake or three feet of snow or even snowmageddon blowing outside. None of that mattered in the casino. People around town might complain about 'casino morals' but she'd learned that, for her, it was a slice of bliss. She dealt the cards, players won and lost, she dealt more cards, and the tips added up.

Did she want this forever? Not a chance. But right now, dealing at the Silver Aces was her best option. Maintenance expenses, equipment upkeep and property taxes didn't go into hibernation after the last leaf walk in the fall.

"Call," one of the men at her table declared with unmistakable excitement and only three cards turned up. There was a rumble of disappointment around the table followed by relatively sincere congratulations as the winner showed his hand.

Evelyn suppressed a smile as the winner gathered his chips. He took his time stacking the chips into his tray and then finally slid out of his seat, tossing a mock salute to the losing players.

Groans and complaints erupted from the remaining players. Everyone wanted a chance to change their luck.

"Know when to quit, that's my motto," the winner said. "There's a song about that right?"

"More than one," she replied.

With a wink, he slid a hundred-dollar chip her way as a tip.

"Thank you. It was a pleasure having you at the Silver Aces." Evelyn delivered the standard response politely when inside she was doing a dance of joy.

When the remaining players were settled again, she pulled the freshly shuffled deck from the automatic shuffler and prepared to deal the next game. She didn't need a clock to know her break was due after this game, her aching feet and back kept time for her. Tonight, she was looking forward to getting to the break room so she could check her phone. She wanted to make sure her dad was all right and, with luck, there would be an email from Tate with new post-storm options for tour times.

"Pardon me. Is it too late to slide in for this hand?"

She shot a quick glance at the poker room host and confirmed the customer was in the right place. Giving the man a nod to take the seat, she waited for him to post his minimum bet and then she dealt him in.

"Evelyn Cotton," he said as the players checked their cards. "Wow. It's really you."

That voice filtered through her senses, a sweet memory and brand new at the same time. Her head snapped up and she was immediately caught in a bright, laser-blue gaze. Those familiar eyes seemed to freeze time, stopping it short and pitching her backward.

Wyatt Jameson.

This was the last place on earth she'd expect to see him. Of course she'd given up on ever seeing him again, period. What had she done so wrong that fate or luck or whatever dumped him at her table? Her gaze swept over the room. Surely there had been another dealer with an open seat.

Somehow, she forced her attention back to the game. Verifying bets on the first round were complete, she turned up three cards in the middle of the table. For the first time since she'd gone solo as a dealer in this room her stomach churned with something just shy of panic.

"How have you been?" he asked after placing his second-round bet.

"Fabulous." The audacity of the man to walk in here and act as if they were old friends who'd simply lost touch.

She dealt the turn, adding the fourth card to the middle of the table. Reading her players, she gave a nod acknowledging one player raising the bet and another player folding. Wyatt added chips, staying in the game.

With an effort, she wrenched her gaze from his. She hadn't seen those stunning eyes since the night they'd graduated high school. Eleven long, lonely years without a word from the guy who'd been her best friend *and* her boyfriend. During those last two years of high school, she'd given him her heart and her virginity, shared all of her dreams and the worst of her fears. She'd bared her soul to him, revealing all of that and her budding expectations for the two of them.

Dealing the river, she turned up the fifth card in the middle of the table and called for final bets.

As each player made a bet or folded, she called for the showdown, less surprised than she should've been when Wyatt won. While her mind whirled over what brought Wyatt back to Deadwood, she cleared the table of cards and chips and reset for the next game.

Growing up had not been easy for him. As his best friend, she'd caught glimpses of the rocky home life he'd endured on a daily basis. Still, in her heart there had been an understanding between them, and she'd been crushed when he'd walked away, with zero explanation.

Eleven years of silence. No letters or calls. He'd simply excised himself from both Deadwood and her in one shocking move. She'd been shattered more than heartbroken. He'd been the one person she'd counted on and confided in and she'd thought...

Well, clearly what she'd thought had been irrelevant.

By some miracle her hands didn't falter in the next deal. Muscle memory was a wonderful thing, she supposed. She should've been focused on the game and the other players, yet one question screeched incessantly through her mind: why was he here?

"What brings you to the Silver Aces this evening, Mr. Jameson," she said, oozing professional courtesy. If they'd met on the street she might have tackled him. She indulged in a quick fantasy of wrapping her hands around his throat until that sexy half-grin disappeared.

"Mr. Jameson? That's my dad's name. You always called me Wyatt." He smiled at the other players. "We went to high school together."

That earned both of them a round of vaguely curious murmurs and glances from the others at the table. Evelyn called for opening bets, motioning to him as she would any other overly-chatty player and moving the game along. The casino only made money when the cards and money were flowing, and the casino was her priority, not unanswerable questions.

~~This time Wyatt lost. She mentally gave Lady Luck a high~~ five. Normally winning or losing only troubled her if a player was rude or belligerent about it. Not this time. As soon as she reached the relative privacy of the breakroom, she was going to give in to the whoop of delight swirling inside her.

Her thoughts might be mildly inappropriate, but no one would know or care. Especially not Wyatt. If he'd cared about her at all, he would've taken a minute to say goodbye before walking out of her life.

Her replacement walked up, timing the changeover perfectly. "That's it for me, gentleman." She smiled at each of the men around her table, including Wyatt, as she gathered her tips, including the chip from Wyatt. "It's been a pleasure and I wish each of you the best of luck here at the Silver Aces."

Doing the job well was far more important, and more mature, than indulging her childish vindictive streak and sticking out her tongue as she walked by her old flame.

Her father hated that she spent the off-season in the casino but without the seasonal work, they would've lost the business five years ago. She'd long ago stopped pointing out that her expansion ideas would put an end to her days of dealing poker. That line of thinking only created more resentment, one thing her personal life didn't need more of, so she cut it short.

There was a petty victory cheer and a dance of joy in her immediate future just as soon as she exited the casino floor.

"Evie?"

She flinched at the sound of the nickname that was used so rarely these days. Of course Wyatt had followed her. Of course he would revert to that old familiarity, sweeping her back to the days when they'd thought they were unstoppable and love would last forever. She walked on, refusing to turn around.

"Can we talk?"

"No." *No, no, no!* The hurt and angry teenager standing guard at the wall she'd build around her heart screamed. He didn't deserve another minute of her time.

"Please?" He fell into step beside her.

Slot machines chimed and jingled all around them. Lights flashed and a ticker high on the wall showed the odds on the upcoming heavyweight boxing match in Las Vegas as well as a tennis tournament in Shanghai.

All of that overwhelming stimulus and yet her senses were dialed in on Wyatt. The natural feel of him striding beside her and the enticing scent of his skin drew her back. Why? After eleven years, neither of those factors should be familiar. They were both different people, two adults on paths that should never intersect.

As the past threatened to swamp her, she considered what *had* changed. His youthful athletic build had filled out. That short beard sculpting his jaw made her fingers tingle with the urge to touch. There was a subtle hitch in his gait that she couldn't quite pin down. He was in a casino, for crying out loud, and playing poker with the skill of a man who did so regularly.

That stopped her. She gathered her composure and schooled her expression as she faced him. She was still on the floor, and therefore still required to maintain an upbeat, positive experience for every guest. Her feelings were irrelevant. The security cameras catching this exchange from every possible angle would only see a valued customer speaking with an employee. Wyatt hadn't taken a threatening position or been rude. She had to respond properly.

"Of course we can talk." She smiled. Cool, detached. "What would you like to discuss, Mr. Jameson?"

Flags of color stained his bold cheekbones and his lips flat-lined, framed by the fashionably scruffy beard.

"Evie—"

"Ms. Cotton," she corrected. "Please. We pride ourselves on our superb and always-appropriate customer service, Mr. Jameson."

"Would you stop?" He crowded her without moving a muscle. "It's me."

Yes, that was exactly why this entire encounter pushed the needle well beyond bizarre. "Are you with the weather service now or something?" It was the only plausible explanation she could think of for Wyatt's appearance in a Deadwood casino.

"What?" He shook his head. "No. There has to be somewhere we can speak privately." His voice rumbled over her, abrading her senses as effectively as his whiskers might. If she gave him the chance to get that close. Which she couldn't do here. Or anywhere.

While holding the professional smile, she shook her head slightly. "Not here."

For her 'here' included the casino, the shops, the restaurants and Deadwood as a whole. She wouldn't go anywhere with him. Couldn't. Being this close, recognizing the flare of heat in his blue gaze, made her want to forget everything he'd put her through and hit a reset switch.

She knew better, had to cling to logic and reason, even if her body was a traitor and didn't care about the way he'd crushed her heart. Yes, he looked good enough to eat and the slight hitch in his step somehow added to the swagger.

"Maybe a manager can be of more assistance," she suggested.

"Damn it, Evie. We were friends."

"We were." She folded her hands at her waist to keep them still while she waited for whatever he had to say.

"I'd like to reconnect." His gaze turned intense and she had the feeling she was supposed to parse out some meaning in what he *wasn't* saying. "At least let me buy you a coffee?"

"No, thank you."

His nostrils flared and his gaze narrowed. "I deserve that."

And more. She smiled when she wanted to snarl. "You deserve the best experience possible at the—"

"Please don't say it." He tucked his hands into his pockets, that blue gaze slicing right through her. "You're at work, I respect that." He glanced over her head, scanning the rows of slot machines.

Old habits, she supposed. At least now he was old enough to be in here legally to look around. His mom had been gone at least three years now. There had been an obituary in the paper and a graveside service. Evelyn hadn't attended the service, but she'd sent a sympathy card and a donation from Cottonwood Adventures.

"When are you off?"

"I'm afraid it's all hands on deck through the storm," she said. It might be true, but she wouldn't know for sure until she actually got to the breakroom. As much as she didn't want to deal with six feet or more of snow, she could use the extra shifts.

"You expect me to believe you're working straight through for the next three days."

"That's right." She dared him to contradict her. "Minimum."

"I see." He rocked back on his heels. "Sounds like an abuse of the work force. Maybe I should call it in."

"Is that what you do now? Go around causing trouble for happy casino employees?"

"You're not happy here," he stated with too much confidence.

Her chin lifted. She wasn't *unhappy* here and she didn't

owe him any explanations about why dealing poker was an important part of her life. "My happiness isn't your concern anymore." She pushed the words through her clenched teeth and tight smile.

He reeled as if she'd slapped him. If only. Maybe she should agree to meet him somewhere. It would have to be somewhere outside and well off the established trails where she could finally let loose with all the pain-filled words and hateful thoughts she'd aimed his way through the years.

That bubble of old hurt and anger swelled in her chest and it took every ounce of willpower to keep her temper locked down while they were in public. At last, the bubble popped, leaving her weary with herself and with him. She was over Wyatt. It had been eleven years. What kind of loser would still be so desperately hung up on a high school boyfriend?

"If you'll excuse me."

"Come with me." Again his gaze swept the area behind her.

"No, thank you." If she didn't know better, she'd think he was part of the casino security team. Whatever he was looking for was none of her business. They weren't a couple anymore. "I really need to take what's left of my break."

His eyes locked with hers. "Evie, please."

A piece of her heart lurched toward him, hammering against the walls she'd built to protect herself. "I can't," she repeated, managing not to rub the pain in her breastbone. "If you're only here because of me, you need to go."

She turned on her heel and strode toward the employees-only door. As if he didn't matter at all.

Once she was through and out of his reach, she leaned against the cool wall. She'd expected walking away from him to feel better. Instead, she wanted to curl up in a corner and cry. Or run back into his arms. Would his embrace be familiar or different? She couldn't deny he'd changed. Grown. Matured. All those things she'd thought she'd done too.

The door swung open as one of her coworkers walked through and she peeked out, startled to see Wyatt still standing there. Almost as if he was keeping watch or waiting for her.

Absurd. He'd leave. He'd go back to the tables. When it came to leaving her behind, Wyatt was a pro.*

THE STORMWATCH SERIES

Holly, the worst winter storm in eighty years...

Holly blows in with subzero temperatures, ice and snow better measured in feet than in inches, and leaves devastation and destruction in its wake. But, in a storm, the weather isn't the only threat—and those are the stories told in the STORMWATCH series. Track the storm through these six chilling romantic suspense novels:

FROZEN GROUND by Debra Webb, Montana
DEEP FREEZE by Vicki Hinze, Colorado
WIND CHILL by Rita Herron, Nebraska
BLACK ICE by Regan Black, South Dakota
SNOW BRIDES by Peggy Webb, Minnesota
SNOW BLIND by Cindy Gerard, Iowa

Get the Books at Amazon

ABOUT THE AUTHOR

USA Today and award-winning author Rita Herron fell in love with books at the ripe age of eight when she read her first Trixie Belden mystery. But she didn't think real people grew up to be writers, so she became a teacher instead. Now she writes so she doesn't have to get a real job!

With over ninety books to her credit, she's penned romantic suspense, romantic comedy, and YA stories, but she especially loves writing dark romantic suspense tales set in southern small towns.

For more on Rita and her titles, visit her at:

www.ritaherron.com. You can also follow her on Facebook and Twitter @ritaherron.

ALSO BY RITA HERRON

Also by Rita Herron

If you liked *Wind Chill* then please write a review on Amazon! You can also contact Rita at www.ritaherron.com and follow her on Facebook and Twitter @ritaherron!

The Keepers Series

Pretty Little Killers (Book 1)

Good Little Girls (Book 2)

Little White Lies (Prequel, Dead Little Darlings, Book 3)

Dead Little Darlings (Book 4)

The Manhunt Series

Safe in His Arms (Book 1)

Safe by His Side (Book 2)

Safe with Him (Book 3)

The Graveyard Falls Series

All the Beautiful Brides (Book 1)

All the Pretty Faces (Book 2)

All the Dead Girls (Book 3)

The Slaughter Creek Series

Before She Dies(Prequel)

~~Dying to Tell (Book 1)~~

✔Her Dying Breath (Book 2)

✔Worth Dying For (Book 3)

✔Dying for Love (Book 4)

The Demonborn Series

Heartless (Book 1)

Mindless (Book 2)

Soulless (Book 3)

Rita's Lighter Side

Marry Me, Maddie

Sleepless in Savannah

Love Me, Lucy

Husband Hunting 101

Here Comes the Bride

There Goes the Groom

Single and Searching

Under the Covers

DON'T MISS

THE EXPLOSIVE SUSPENSE SERIES

A ground-breaking, fast paced 4-book suspense series that will keep you turning pages until the end. Reviews describe BREAKDOWN as "unique," "brilliant" and "the best series of the year." The complete series includes **the dead girl** by Debra Webb, **so many secrets** by Vicki Hinze, **all the lies** by Peggy Webb and **what she knew** by Regan Black. You'll want all four books of the thrilling BREAKDOWN series!

Made in the USA
Coppell, TX
22 September 2020

38594652R00155